Copyright 6-26-15

1-2597867701

Thank you for selecting Bodhi Two, a Black Hole. Ana and her crew are forced through a black hole. Now they must face what is on the other side. This story will bring to light many philosophies.
Bodhi other books:

Bodhi One:	Aliens
Bodhi Two:	Black Hole
Bodhi Three:	Asteroid
Bodhi Four:	Earthstar
Bodhi Five:	Alien War
Bodhi Six:	The Blackness
Bodhi Seven:	The New Planet
Bodhi Eight:	Rose The Warrior

"Ana" A very intense story

A young Jewish girl (14 years) survives the Nazi prison camps, love, and war, written in narrative poetic style.

"Detective Harriet Brown," a series (4 books).

A pampered, sensitive young lady suddenly finds her world upside down and must now struggle to survive.

"Buffalo Boy,"

A young man of thirteen is cast away from his village and forced to live with the buffalo. "Lucky Seven" A young minister goes to Viet Nam and receives the gift of healing, and then loses it. It is a story of redemption. A very powerful story.

"Rose Stories (16 Books)

The story takes place in southern Alabama along the Tensaw River in the year 1830. Rose lives a very sheltered life until she reached the age of twelve when her adventures begin taking the riverboat with its boiler about to explode down the Mississippi River. The adventure continues when her family moves to the Great Plains (Midwest). She finds herself alone, deserted by her family thousands of miles from civilization with an unbalanced Army Captain trying to kill her.

Bodhi Two
Black Hole

By Christopher Charles

Contents

Prologue One

The story takes place on a Starship moving through the black void of outer space. Twelve star-bases are stretched out through the solar system. Ten of them are orbiting existing planets or moons of planets. The last two are drifting in their own orbit just inside the sun's gravitational pull. The next great adventure will be the push through deep space in the attempt to reach the planets of another solar system.

Our probes indicate the presence of possible life on these planets, but it may not be permitted. Certainly not until man learns the concept of no time in the space continuum will he be able to do much more than commit people to the long duration of animated suspension.

On Earth, the religious centers dominated the political and social structures. Even the scientific community acknowledged there was a heaven and hell. In response to this, massive amounts of money were allocated for space exploration at the exclusion of any paranormal studies.

The thought of other dimensions filled with living 'Beings' never did sit well with the hard-core scientist. To accept the concept of God creating the universe wasn't a bad trade off if it meant unlimited funds and a work force to explore the dominion of God (i.e. space exploration). They didn't have an answer for the creator of the big bang anyway. What compressed such a massive amount of energy to begin with, they did not know. They will accept God doing it. Evidence showing the universe was somehow increasing its mass did bother them, but someday the understanding of the working creative forces in the galaxies would be allowed.

Paranormal studies were being eliminated. Only a few cults existed, and these were under pressure from all sides. Called quackery, the scientific community did not dare touch them. Of course, the technique of taking people across the veil with hypnosis to explore the inner world was all the devils' work. People long dead channeling through innocent sensitives' was all fake to ruin people's hopes and take their money.

To say the population was shielded from the truth was an understatement, but this may be a blessing. Simple explanations for events occurring in the universe were easier to accept, and less disturbing to the psychic.

Deviations from the quote 'normal' were cured with the Psych Tanks. This was the process of using computerize probes to change the brain waves of an individual to relieve him of his madness. Many paranormal activists came out completely normal after being exposed to one of these sessions.

The concept of living energy moving through the universe, expressing a personality, was beyond the present scientific thinking. The thought of all energy evolving from one such small existence after it bloomed, then learning to create and expand into our present universe was not attainable.

Though the concept followed the religious idea more, the

scientific community was not about to buy it, always liking the big bang theory. The religious centers bending to the scientist here was the healing catalyst between the two.

This did not stop the universe from expanding outward to replace the eternal darkness, creating energy, giving birth to new things, and learning seemingly endlessly. Yet, the overall conscious wondered, was this done before? Letting his conscious drift back, all he could pick up was the bloom. It was a birth of sorts before he learned to create. He found no one around to teach or direct his course. Only him stumbling through the eternal darkness, alone, making mistakes until he learned.

He did pick up a faint present that another did exist. He could only speculate. Yes, he could feel events changing in his space of no time that may tell him more.

1 The Black Pod

Alone black woman floated free in her spacesuit. Her eyes, staring out into the blackness, tried hard to perceive some light in this night without end. She felt so alone. The stars had disappeared. She could only feel the blackness pushing in on her. Her throat was on the verge of screaming, but her training held, allowing her to drift further into this black quagmire.

Suddenly she saw something. Her mind didn't register it, but her throat did, allowing her to scream. The sound jerked her awake. She sat up quickly, looked around slowly. It was her nightmare again. It was the second one tonight. She should have gone into the Psych Tank the first time, but she didn't have time.

Captain of the Star Ship Neoann, Ana Mc Clure had been combating one problem after another. Mostly it has been the crew. They were all on edge, extremely nervous from something, becoming progressively worse the longer they remained here.

Her ship has been circling a large dark energy field. At first, she thought it was a black hole because it whirled slowly, but the ship's sensors said otherwise. It was looking more like a dark cloud with the mass of an asteroid, except none of their electronic probes could penetrate it. Even their drones lost contact and control immediately upon penetration. They had preset directions in the drones' computers, but none of them returned. They must have run into something solid in the middle.

Awake, she swung out of bed, and slipped into her uniform. She kicked the floor plate, the bed disappeared into the wall. "Might as well," she thought. She wouldn't be going back to sleep. Going out the sliding door, she headed for the observation deck.

She walked fast to wear off some of her tension. She didn't slow until she entered the dome. The seamless Plexiglas gave one the illusion they were in space without a suit. Soft floating couches were anchored in the middle of the half done. This allowed one to see nothing, but the darkness speckled with stars. Except now a large black mass crowded the other stars out.

This was her favorite spot. A place she liked to be alone in to collect her thoughts. It was empty! Good! This time of night it usually was, especially now with everyone spooked over the dark mass. She would be glad when they could leave it.

Finding the very center chair, she pulled herself up strapping in. There was only partial gravity here. She didn't like her body floating up. Laying back, she looked at the large black mass. It took up most of the viewing space with this close of an orbit. Nothing ever changed. The black mass just hung there absorbing their probes.

Scientists on space station Alpha Twelve picked it up first. It would pass through the outer portion of earth's solar system in two months. Her ship was ordered to investigate. She was to establish orbit and learn what it was, but after two days it remained a mystery.

Frustrated, she pressed the button whirling the observation hall to the other side of the ship. Actually, the hall didn't move only the outside cameras switched. Yes, this was only a projection on the Plexiglas, but she liked to think it was real.

"You didn't like the other view?" A voice behind her asked.

Startled, she sat up quickly. She was not alone! "Where, where are you?"

"Behind you," the voice replied.

Whirling, she saw an older man in his late fifties, "Doctor Parker, what are you doing here?"

"More to the point, why are you here?"

"Couldn't sleep! Thought I would enjoy the scenery."

"The dream again, huh?"

She nodded falling back on the chair. "More like a nightmare."

"Most of our crew has them. Must be coming from that thing outside. How much longer are we going to stay here?"

"Until we find out something!" She said firmly. "I can't go back and tell them what they already know."

"They don't know your crew and you are being affected."

"And you?"

"Yes, and me. Maybe you ought to take a bigger orbit. It might be healthier."

"No, we'll be taking a closer one," she said matter of factually.

"Closer?" Shouting, "Good lord, girl, do you want to fill every psych tank between here and Alpha One?"

"Don't panic, Doctor, it'll be you, Henderson and myself. We'll be taking the shuttle. We're going at 0800. You better be getting some sleep, this could be a long one."

Parker gave her a hard stare. Then he pulled himself up out of his chair muttering, "I'm no space jockey. I don't like that thing messing up my mind. I have patients here that need me whole."

"Sorry, Doctor, I'll be needing you there. I'm going inside."

Startled, he turned around. "Did I hear you right?"

Softly she said, "Yes, I'm going inside! There is no other way."

"I think that thing has warped your mind, ma'am. Pull this ship out of orbit a few days, then decide."

"Yes," she said calmly. "A bigger orbit is good, but we are still going at 0800."

"Damn! There's no reasoning with you, ma'am."

"I'm aware of your feelings, Doctor, but you will have Mr. Henderson. I am the only expendable one here, and the only one I can ask."

"You think this is going to make you some kind hero or something?"

"Doctor, you know better."

"Yes, but it's my job to probe all areas." He turned and walked out mumbling something, but she could no longer hear.

She lay back in her chair knowing there would be no sleep for her tonight. Letting her mind wander, she tried to evaluate why she was taking such a risk. It was not the hero thing. No, it went much deeper.

What she told Parker held. There was no other way to get information. They were not about to accept a psychological study of her crew. She tried to make herself believe that, but it was her dream. This wasn't the first time in her life she has had it. Always the same, she would wake up before she entered it. There, she said it! Something was inside that black mass so frightening her senses wouldn't allow her to perceive it.

She has never told Psych about it in the past, and the darkness phobia never came up in anything else. Yes, she told Parker two days ago, but he assumed it was a recent occurrence, blaming it on the black mass. Most of the crew has been affected by it, but this dream has been occurring since she was a child.

It was like this was her destiny. Call it fate, coincidence, or whatever they liked, but she has been led to this position at this time. Now she had to face it! What was on the other side of the darkness? 0800 tomorrow she would find out.

In her trans-like state she heard the familiar footsteps looking for her. Judy Laury, her Yeoman, was very pretty and delicate. The kind of woman she knew she could never be. Judy didn't really belong in space, but her sensitivity was indispensable. Softly she said, "Over here!"

The light footsteps followed the voice. She stood waiting.

"Did Parker send you?"

"No, Mr. Henderson thought you might need some company."

"Not tonight, Judy. I think I would rather be alone."

Judy wiped a tear from her eye knowing Ana couldn't see her in the dark. "You … You won't be coming back, will you?"

Sitting up, Ana asked, "Who told you that?"

"Mr. Henderson! He said the probes didn't."

"Probes don't think! We don't know what's in there, so we can't program them."

Judy ran to her letting her tears flow. "Don't go!" She pleaded. "Please don't go! There's something awful in there. I know there is!"

Ana took her in her arms and patted her back. When she began to feel better, Ana asked, "You've been having dreams."

"Yes, it's…It's alive! It wants our ship." Her tears turned to sobs and caused her chest to heave up and down.

Rubbing her gently, Ana tried to calm her. "Now, now, it's only a black cloud mass. This is no way for my yeoman to behave."

Slowly standing, Judy held her sobs in. "Sorry ma'am, I didn't mean to fall apart."

"It's okay. Did you pick up anything else?"

"Just the ominous feelings everyone else has been having."

"Thank you, then that will be enough."

Judy looked at her Captain, hesitated, and said softly, "I…I would like to stay."

"Yes, I know, but not tonight. I want to be alone."

"Yes ma'am!" Judy said, and turned slowly. She started to walk, but this quickly became a run when her tears returned.

Ana watched her for a moment, and then she fell back on the couch. Yes, a very sensitive young lady. This black nothingness has been especially hard on her. It would have been nice to have some company, but she must prepare her mind for 0800. She wanted to survive, but she was also aware of the probabilities.

She thought about praying to God, but she didn't really believe one existed. Her mind remembered the biblical God preached to her as a child. Especially the sermons containing hell, fire and brimstone! She had images of people suffering and mashing their teeth. "No, this is not for her," she said to herself. "No God would be cruel enough to allow such a place to exist."

Letting her mind relax, she became lost in the array of stars. What would God look like if he commanded all the energy she saw in front of her? She asked herself. No, only a small petty God would think of a hell and take pleasure in punishing people. A warped one at that, she thought.

Feeling more relaxed, she allowed her mind to follow this train of thought. There might be life after death, but it certainly wouldn't be in a hell. Slowly this became less important.

Whoever created all of this has a greater purpose, she thought. Yes, and she was part of it. Otherwise why would she be here? This was no accidental encounter, but one she sought.

Her mind was drifting becoming lost in the sea of stars. She allowed the music to take her inside. Briefly wondering who turned it on, but the soft footsteps told her as she passed over into sleep.

The next morning at 0800, Mr. Henderson, a big muscular man with a high forehead, maneuvered the shuttle out of the ship's bay doors. His lips were tight. He didn't like this mission. She was going inside for what? Science? No, it was more. Something personal and she wasn't talking. "E.T.A., two minutes," he announced in an automatic voice.

"Thank you, Mr. Henderson," Ana said taking one last look at the ship. She watched it leave orbit. No sense in exposing them.

Parker looked up. "We should be going with them."

"And miss all of this?"

"What? Watch you commit suicide?"

"There is always risk, Doctor."

Mr. Henderson, not turning, said, "Some are not necessary!"

"This one is, believe me!" She said adding the extra emotion.

"Then you better be getting your suit on, ma'am," Mr. Henderson said with an irritated twinge in his voice. "We're here!"

She released her seatbelt, pulled herself aft. A few minutes later she returned with her suit on.

"Wait a sec.," Henderson said after he helped her strap on the thruster pack. He reached into the locker pulling out a large spool of wire. "I'm attaching this."

"What is it?"

"Wire! Plain old wire!"

"Where did you find that?"

"Don't ask! It will let us keep contact after we lose the com."

"Good idea!"

"When you run out of wire, you come back! Agreed?"

"It sounds reasonable, but how far can I go in?"

"Two hundred yards!"

"That may not be enough!"

"It's enough this time!" Henderson said in a firm voice. "You lose this wire, and we lose you. You know what happened to the drones."

"Yes, attach it please." In her mind she knew it was not going to be long enough. What was inside was much deeper.

Mr. Henderson attached the wire to her communication pack, then placed the spool in a special device he had constructed. After he had threaded the wire through another communication pack in the airlock, he climbed back inside. Going to the com., he said, "Easy does it and the spool will stay with you."

She stepped into the airlock. She felt the hatch close behind her and the air being sucked out. The outer hatch opened. She turned, gave thumbs up pushing off from the shuttle. After floating free a moment, she gave her thruster pack a short burst. She headed out for the darkness. Her mind remembered Judy's warning. "It's alive. It wants our ship." She has relied on her sensitivity before. It has always proven correct. Taking her ship out of harms' way took care of the one threat, but the other, "It's alive!" How will she deal with that? What was alive? This black mass, or the nightmare inside?

Her thoughts suddenly were shattered by Mr. Henderson's voice. "Twenty seconds to entry! Remember! Slow! I don't want the wire breaking."

All she could see was the blackness. She had no idea how close she was. The sudden entry surprised her. She felt the black mass flowing around her suit. She felt cold even through the heated suit. "I'm in," she said in a quiet voice.

"Yes, we've already lost you on the com. Only the wire is working," Mr. Henderson replied. "Slow! Remember slow! Your computer is keeping your coordinates, but I'm not sure how accurate it is."

"It's cold, Mr. Henderson! Very cold! I can't see a thing!"

"You're changing course again! What are you doing?"

"Nothing! There must be a current in here. Want me to correct for it."

"No, you're already coming back, but it's taking more wire."

"Maybe it knows what you're trying to do and doesn't like it."

"Just currents, ma'am! Just currents!"

"Where's your humor, Mr. Henderson? I'm giving it another burst." She held the thruster button for two seconds, and felt the pack drive her forward.

"You're in one hundred yards," Mr. Henderson said.

"It's colder, I have the heater up to maximum, but I'm still freezing."

"You could run into ice. Could be what's in the center."

"With this density it should be hotter. I think we've miscalculated something here."

Doctor Parker interrupted, "How is it affecting you?"

"Ominous, doctor! Ominous!"

"Have you tried the outside light?"

"Yes, but I turned it off. The stuff is too thick reflecting it. I can feel it moving around the suit. Some of it is thicker. It actually pushes the suit in a bit, then moves on."

"Interesting, but how are you doing?"

"If you don't mind being in a sea of darkness, and feeling something crawling all over you, it isn't bad, but to answer your question, apprehensive, very apprehensive!"

"Scared, Captain?"

"Maybe, Doctor, maybe!"

Mr. Henderson broke in saying, "Time to reverse your pack. You're running out of wire."

"But we haven't learned anything!" The tone in her voice said she wanted more time. "I think we should…"

Mr. Henderson interrupting, "Ma'am, we agreed on the two hundred yards. We can get more wire later for a deeper probe."

"You're right Mr. Henderson reversing now." Actually, she was glad to be coming back. There was more here. She could feel it, but her mind had all the darkness it wanted. She didn't think it would be this bad.

Suddenly she felt herself moving faster. She had not turned the thruster pack on yet.

Mr. Henderson was screaming in her ear. "The wrong way! The wrong way! Change directions! You're running out of wire!"

She tried to turn the pack, but each time the current caused her to tumble a different direction. "Mr. Henderson, I'm tumbling! I'm caught in a strong current! I can't get my direction!"

"Hit the thrusters now! You're out of wire! You're out of .."

She did not hear Mr. Henderson's plea, only the sound of the wire snapping free from the com. "Mr. Henderson! Mr. Henderson! Do you copy?"

It was a useless gesture. She allowed herself to tumble. Her lifeline gone, she floated free and alone in her black nightmare. Her mind wanted to panic, but her training held. Calming herself, she thought, "I still have the computer, but first I have to stop this tumbling and get control!"

She gave the thrusters a couple of burst. Slowly the tumbling stopped allowing her a moment to survey the damage. She brought her arms out of the suit, turned the internal light on. Checking her computer, it wasn't working. She reached up to touch it. It felt frozen! She…She was lost in the moving black current with less than twelve hours of air.

"Hold it! Get a grip!" She yelled to herself. "I still have the thruster pack." Angling the suit, she gave it a long burst and drifted. Thirty minutes later she was out of the current, but what side, out or in? Giving it another burst, she picked up speed. Now all she could do was let fate work.

If she chose the correct side, she would be out in a few

minutes. Suddenly she felt herself falling, or was she being pulled? No, she was going in a circular motion picking up speed. It felt like… "A whirlpool!" She was being sucked down! The pressure, increasing, was taking her inside!

No wonder the pods never came back, she thought. The mass was alive with activity. Yet it seemed so peaceful and static on the outside. She will be lost forever in this abyss of quicksilver! She will die in less than twelve hours by suffocating in her own suit.

No longer trying to fight her way out, she allowed the whirlpool to take her down. Even if she were to hit the thruster pack a full ten minutes, she wouldn't know which direction. She had to be a mile inside this mass. It could be a hundred miles judging by the speed she was moving.

Actually, all she felt was the pressure on her suit. Pulling, the suction almost sucked it off her body. Then when it reached the critical point, it would ease off. It seemed to be reading her mind. "Is it taking me somewhere?"

Suddenly realizing what these thoughts implied, she yelled, "No! No! I didn't mean that!" Quickly she checked the oxygen mixture. It appeared correct, but she added more of the oxygen. Maybe her mind was lacking the precious gas. She decided she would be rational up to the very end.

Hours later nothing had changed. She was still in her elevator going down or in. Maybe she was going up, but she doubted it. Actually, she was dreaming someone was caressing her. It was more like a loving emotion a mother would give to her child.

Suddenly the scene changed. She was still spinning slowly, but now she was moving head first. The darkness seemed to be lighter. It was her nightmare again or was she now awake seeing it happened. She felt her throat getting ready to scream, but nothing came out. She was in a tunnel moving rapidly toward a reddish orange flame at the other end.

Picking up speed, she was going to smash into it. The temperature changed. She could feel the suit's protective covering giving way to the heat. "She would be burnt alive!"

Hitting the flaming mass, she screamed! The sound consumed all of her 'Being', but this time she didn't wake up. She kept her eyes close until the heat subsided. Then slowly she opened them and looked around. She was still alive! She didn't understand why. She thought she would be dead. Maybe she was.

She was floating in a sea of colors with the greenish orange being the dominant. She was in a current with other pieces of fabric. These varied from thick dark green to thin wispy strands of yellow. Some large ones were bumping into her similar to the dark mass, but now she could see them. The current was moving her through a large void filled with a gaseous light green substance.

She was still in a tunnel of sorts. It even appeared to have definite sides separating the current from the void. The colors continued to whirl around her. She was fascinated by a particular long wispy piece of fabric that began wrapping itself around her.

She had her hands inside working the computer trying to determine the type of gas she was in. Suddenly the wispy arm moved though her head plate. Shocked and surprised, she watched the fabric wrap itself around her body.

Looking up, the view plate was open! "How did that happen?" She reached up to close it, but the face plate wouldn't move. Confused, she held her breath. Fear kept her from breathing the poison gas. Desperately she fought the fabric suffocating her.

She needed to breathe! She needed to breathe now! The suit's gas indicator light registered green. It was breathable! Could she trust the light? Was she hallucinating?

Something was stopping her from closing the hatch, or was she opening it? The wispy arm reached through the open hatch wrapping itself around her head. "That just happened, didn't it? Isn't that what opened the plate? No, her own hand did that!" Confused! The oxygen, it was draining from her body! She had to breathe in! Giving up, she took a deep breath to let it kill her quickly. She was tired of the cat and mouse game.

Slowly she let the air out. She seemed to be all right. It was breathable. Reaching down, she turned off the suit's oxygen to let her lungs fill with this new gas.

The wispy green filament continued to press moving tighter around her head. She began to feel dizzy. She felt a sharp pain in her forehead, then blackness.

2 Paradise

She woke up slowly trying to focus her eyes. How long has she been out? She didn't know. She felt cold. A breeze was hitting her face. In the background she could hear water breaking over rocks. Working her eyes, she needed to focus! Was she at the beach?

Slowly sitting, she felt her long hair fall over her shoulder. Who let her hair down? Reaching to throw it back, she felt her arm and back. Her clothes were gone! Touching more, she was naked! Pushing hard she forced her eyes open.

Quickly she looked around. Yes! Yes! She was on the beach. "Her beach!" She shouted. The one at home, but this was not home! The sky seemed different. Where was she? Why was she here? Her strength was coming back. She felt better. She could stand. Her legs didn't like the gravity. She could feel the deep pain wanting to surface from her underused muscles.

Working her legs, she noticed something familiar laying on a sand bar. It was on the other side of the small lagoon in front of her. The ocean, coming in beyond that, was breaking over the rocks. It would reach it soon. She knew the water coming in would cover the sandbar. It would fill the lagoon with cold water like it always has.

The dark object was important. She felt it. A part of her somehow. She could not let the water take it out. Forgetting the pain in her legs, she ran for the lagoon. She took the water to her waist, dove smoothly, and went into her power stroke.

A minute later she was on the other beach. It looked like a body or something. Closer, it seemed familiar. It was a spacesuit! "My spacesuit!" She gasped falling beside it. Her mind was confused. Why was her spacesuit here? Who would have left it on the beach? She didn't bring her suit home, or did she?

Reaching inside, she found her uniform. Suddenly she felt naked. Quickly she pulled her suit on. "How did she get here?" Forcing her mind to remember, she was the captain of a starship. Yes, the darkness, she was hopelessly lost, sucked into this whirling black hole. The burning flames, yes, she went through the burning flames.

"That must be it," she thought. "I'm dead!" The thought struck a deep nerve. Maybe she was in heaven. Heaven was the place you liked the most. Yes, yes, whirling around, "Oh what a wonderful place this is," she said aloud.

A big breaker came in lifting the suit off the sand. She watched it floating out a few seconds, then she ran after it. For some reason she could not let it go. Pulling hard, she found the suit to be heavy without zero gravity. She had it high up on the beach, but it wasn't good enough.

It took her another twenty minutes before she had it safe up on dry land. Feeling better and breathing easier, she walked back to the sand bar. It was almost completely covered with water. In some places the water was spilling over into the lagoon on the other side.

She waded out without caring about her uniform. Fitting like a workout suit, it was made to get wet and dry quickly. She looked across the water. She saw her familiar island six hundred yards offshore.

Remembering, yes, she used to swim there. It was her magical 'Treasure Island.' Feeling the urge to do so again, she waded further out into the surf. Timing the breakers, she dove into the receding water. She went through the next breaker and found herself free of the turbulence.

She swam hard for twenty minutes then lifted her head to check her direction. The island wasn't there! She started to panic! "Did I swim pass it?" She asked herself. Turning, she could not see the land or the sand bar. Only water! Whirling, "Nothing but water!" She was stranded in mid ocean! "Easy! Easy! Calm yourself, think! Think!" She said to herself.

Yes, she would swim back the same direction for twenty

minutes. Maybe she was a faster swimmer then she thought. She flipped over. Putting her head down, she went into her power stroke. After ten minutes she wanted to raise her head, but no, she would swim the full twenty minutes. She continued to count her strokes knowing she completed one every five seconds.

Another five minutes passed. She wanted to stop. No, she kept going! She didn't want to change anything. Lifting her head would mess up the momentum. This had to be done right. Finally reaching twenty minutes, she lifted her head quickly. She should be in front of the sand bar, but…But nothing…Only more water.

She flipped over on her back to rest. "No sense in swimming more," she thought. "There is no place to go." She remembered her mother warning her about swimming so far. "It's dangerous young lady! Anything could happen to you. A fog bank could roll in."

Suddenly she felt cold. Rolling over on her stomach, she looked around. A heavy fog had settled in. "Did her thoughts do this?" She asked allowed. Maybe the land was here, but she wasn't seeing it. Where did that thought come from? Putting her head down, she began to swim for the beach again.

She did two strokes, found her fingers digging into sand. Quickly she stood finding herself in two feet of water. She had been laying here on her back all this time in two feet of water. The land was here under her feet. She was standing on the sandbar.

Shaken, she did not understand what was happening. She walked on top of the sandbar. She was no longer cold. The sun was drying her uniform quickly. Sun? Turning around, the fog was gone. "Things happen so fast here," she said aloud. "I must control my thoughts."

Whirling back around, she could see the land on the other side of the lagoon. Feeling better, she dove into the warm water. She swam quickly to the other side, but she kept her head out of the water in a lifesaving stroke. She didn't want to chance losing the land again.

"That must be it," she thought. "The water coming in covered the sand dune and more of the beach on the other side. Then the fog bank came in. No wonder I didn't see anything," her mind reasoned, but the rumbling in the pit of her stomach said otherwise.

Walking up the beach, she checked her spacesuit. Yes, it was still here. That was real! Remembering the island, she turned quickly, looked out across the water. Yes, yes, it was there again. "How did she miss it? Did she swim the wrong direction? Maybe it was not really there."

She would think about it tomorrow. Everything seemed so confusing. She was tired and hungry. "Yes, it must be time to go home," she thought. "See mom and tell her about it." Home! The thought finally registered. Which way was it? Looking around, she saw the water was in front of her and the sand dunes behind. Home was a quarter of a mile across the dunes, but she could not move.

Fear held her! She didn't understand. What was she afraid of, her mother? No, she knew she was dead, but if this was heaven she would be here.

She didn't want to know, but her feet began moving over the dunes. Her fear increased, she had to find out! Running, she picked up speed. Easily reaching the top of the first sand dune, she started down. She had been over these dunes a thousand times. Going up the last sand dune, she knew her house should be fifty yards beyond at the tree line. For some reason this dune was higher than the others.

When she was half way up the sand dune, she stopped to catch her breath. Turning, she expected to see the ocean, but all she saw was more sand dunes. Something was not right. Where was she? Suddenly frightened she ran the rest of the way up the sand dune.

On top she looked around quickly. She should see her house from here. At the very least the ocean, but all she saw were more sand dunes going on endlessly. Dropping to her knees, she realized what her stomach already knew. She was trapped here! Any direction out only brought her difficulty.

The sun felt hot bearing down on her. She wanted a drink, but none was to be had. Forcing herself to her feet, she started down the sand dune following her footsteps. She knew where they would lead. She didn't dare take her eyes off the trail of imprints, or she would be lost forever.

Ten minutes later, sure enough, she was back at her beach, her little piece of heaven. She found her favorite spot high up on the beach. She watched the water receding back off the sand bar. With her head on her knees and her arms holding her legs, she tried to think. "What's happening? The turn of the tide isn't due for another three hours, yet there it goes," she said aloud. "I can't seem to leave this place. Every time I do, I lose sight of it."

Inside she knew another fear. "Wander too far," she thought, "I may not be able to come back, and be forced to wonder the endless sand dunes." The water was no better! She was trapped here. "No, my mind is," she said to herself. Suddenly she realized this wasn't heaven. This was boredom. "How many times can one swim in the warm lagoon?" She asked herself. "How long can she sit here and do nothing?"

She missed the action, the unknown, people and their problems, especially the competition. There may not be any people here, but there were plenty of the unknowns. Yes, I will explore the area, she decided. I will leave my precious sanctuary and take my chances.

While the idea formed, she was moving her feet back towards the sand dune. She would see what was on the other side. She stopped to give her little oasis one last look. Swallowing the lump developing in her throat, she started for her house. This time she would go all the way.

Ten minutes later she was still walking. She was moving faster now that she had lost sight of the ocean. Finally, she could see her house. It was exactly as she had pictured it. Running the last hundred yards, she boomed through the front door, yelling, "Mom! Mom! I'm home!"

Her mind told her she would not find her, but the sound of her voice made her feel better. She ran through the house quickly. The same as she had left it years ago, but her mother wasn't there.

Feeling hungry, she went to the refrigerator. Hoping to find something, she swung the door wide. "It…It's empty," she said aloud. "More than that, the refrigerator was fading." Quickly she looked around. The whole house was disappearing! Racing outside, she saw everything fading. The dunes, the house, the trees, everything! A greenish haze replaced them. She looked for some solid ground praying she didn't fall through.

A voice asked, "Why do you wish to leave the place I have prepared for you?"

Whirling around, "Who said that? I didn't leave anywhere! This is not my house!"

"Very well if you do not wish to remain here, then I will cast you out!"

"Where are you? Cast me out of what? You mean this heaven?"

The voice didn't answer.

"Show yourself!" Ana demanded. "I don't like taking orders from a spook! I said show yourself!"

"Oh, very well." A small field of greenish orange energy the size of a basketball began to form and float in front of her.

Ana backed away. "What are you?"

"I am the Creator of All Things," the energy answered.

"You're…You're God?"

"If you wish to call me this, I am your God."

The 'Being' was talking in her head telepathically. The voice sounded human. "How did you know my language?"

"I know your mind, that is all I need," the being replied. "Now our souls must join. We will become one in the spirit."

"What do you mean, one? I don't let just anyone become part of me. You're Alien! You stay what you are, and I will stay what I am."

"If you will not accept me, become one with my 'Being', then I will cast you into eternal damnation."

"I didn't mean that!" She said. Now realizing, she may have put herself into a more serious situation. "Don't cast me out of heaven. Can't we…?" She started to say as her feet began to sink. She looked up at the hovering 'Being'. She could feel it laughing. "Hey!" Ana yelled, "Let's talk about this! Why do you need me?"

"It's not you, it's your body! I want your body! Either we become one and share it, or I'll leave you here and take it," the 'Being' said, "You decide!"

She didn't hear more as she continued to fall deeper into the green mire. She left the 'Being' somewhere above. "She wants my body! Why?" She asked herself. She remembered Judy's warning. "The ship, the 'Being' wanted the ship!" It started to make sense. She had to get out of here! "She's not dead! She's inside a living 'Being'!" There! She said it! "I'm inside a living being!" She shouted.

The knot in her stomach said she was correct. A small rumble passed through her body. She needed her suit, she needed out of here or kill herself trying.

She felt herself tumbling. Spreading her arms, she managed to slow before her back struck something hard. It hurt! She couldn't move. She decided to lie there until the pain had run its course. She must be at the bottom of something. The surface felt flat and hard. The haze lifted enough to allow her to see her surroundings. Actually, she smelt them first. "Sulfur, poisonous sulfur springs," She yelled. She was beside a pothole of boiling sulfur water.

Rolling to her left, she was quickly on her feet. She looked around. The place was full of potholes going out of sight over the horizon. "Another illusion?" She asked herself. "Can she be sure?"

She heard a rumble from the boiling spring in front of her.

Deep, it became louder. "It's going to blow!" She started running. Behind her she heard the hot sulfur water blowing out of the hole. Any second she would feel the hot water. To the right she saw a low hill with a cave of sorts going deeper underground.

She dove for it allowing her body to roll once when she reached the mouth of the cave. Some scalding water managed to reach her left leg sending pain shooting through her body. She came up in a sitting position breathing hard.

She didn't wait to check her leg. Probably a second-degree burn, she thought, but there was nothing she could do about it here. She pushed herself up. She decided to stay in the cave. She had no trouble seeing. The glowing greenish yellow slime on the walls emitted a strange light. It allowed her to walk easily. A feeling deep inside was telling her not to trust this. She knew the sulfur geysers outside were probably dissolving. The burning pain from the boiling water was real. She could be hurt. That proved she was alive!

Ten minutes into the cave a grinding noise caught her attention. Turning back, she saw the tunnel closing off behind her. More than closing it was moving towards her. Pressing, it tied to force her forward. She stood watching it approach. The wall of greenish orange became brighter and hotter. "Maybe this isn't real," she said aloud. She could feel the heat radiating from it.

Enough, she couldn't take more. She turned running the

only direction she could gaining on the wall. Slowing to listen, she could hear the wall moving behind her. Picking up speed, she put more distance between it. She could feel her long hair bouncing on her shoulders and staying in rhythm. "How long is the tunnel? What happens when it ends?" Looking back, the wall was gaining. She dug in harder.

Suddenly the tunnel stopped. In front of her she saw another wall of the green glowing gelatin. She heard the wall behind her grinding closer. Panicking, she looked up. "No escape there," she said, "Only more of the same." Turning, she faced the moving wall coming around the bend. It started toward her. Slowly backing, her eyes riveted on the glowing greenish orange gelatin, oozing over the stone. It was turning yellow becoming hotter.

The other walls began moving. Evened the ceiling was closing in on her. "I'll be burnt alive!" She screamed closing her eyes. "Please God! Not this! I'll do anything!" The rumbling walls continued to press. She could feel the searing heat. She smelt something! "My hair!" She screamed. "It's burning my hair!" She was going to die! She knew it! Her throat was screaming, but she didn't hear it. The pain took her out into the cool darkness.

3 The Tests

She woke up smelling sulfur flumes. Her eyes were not focused, but she could feel with her hands. "I must still be in hell, and…And alive!" She said to herself. "Yes, I am alive." Then she yelled up at the fog above her. "I don't care anymore! You hear me! I don't care!" She refused to get up and entertain this…This god!

Suddenly the ground shook! Instantly her mind registered an Earthquake! The rumblings shook her 'Being'. Quickly she sat up forcing herself to focus. She started to roll to her right, when she found herself looking down into the hole of a volcano. She could see the boiling lava threatening to erupt. A new fear flooded her 'Being'. She wanted to scream but held it back. She forced the fear into anger. "You fiend!" She yelled. "I'm not going into that!"

The input of epinephrine turned her tired body into action. Planting her feet, she started to roll to her left, when the rock beneath her suddenly cracked. She found herself dropping into the crater. Flinging her arms out, she managed to reach a protruding rock. Hanging on tight, she was saved temporarily.

Without enough strength to swing her legs up, she dangled, awaiting her fate. Below, she heard the broken off piece of rock splash into the molten lava. It sent a small cloud of steam up. Her mind wondered how big of a cloud her body would make?

She heard a voice in her head say, "Give me your body!" Anger replacing hopelessness, she gave her body one last push, bringing her legs up to wrap around the rock. "You can't have it!" "You hear! You can't!"

Cruel laughter filled her head. The volcano rumbled again dislodging her rock from the wall of stone. She felt herself falling until something snagged the back of her uniform stopping her descent. She had no idea how it happened, but she found herself hanging over the volcano looking straight down into the jaws of hell.

"Give me your body," the voice said.

"No!" She didn't say it convincingly. She also knew it meant her death and heard the back of her uniform give way. She didn't scream passing into the blackness.

Opening her eyes, she found herself falling backward through a flaming tunnel. Out of reflex she flipped herself over to see the fire coming off the walls trying to consume her. Their fiery tongues reached out singing her hair. She watched it take parts of her uniform, yet she was alive.

She tried to think. She knew she had only seconds before she would be tested again. Yes, the 'Being' wanted her body. Yes, she could be hurt. Her pain was real. The burnt off hair was real. That has been consistent. So has her survival in all of the encounters. Maybe, just maybe she could change that.

She started to deliberately fling herself into the flames. Each time they would move back. Yes, the flames were meant to hurt, not kill her. She allowed this knowledge to work through feeling the power emerging with this discovery. She began to move faster, daring anything to stop her.

The flames quickly changed to cool greenish water flowing deeper inside. It was taking her somewhere, but it didn't matter! She had her weapon!

Suddenly the tunnel disappeared. She found herself floating in a small walled city. It appeared very old, sort of out of sync. Her feet felt something solid. She could stand. Looking around she was in a courtyard of sorts. Surrounding her were low hanging stone buildings with large wooden support beams. Behind this stood an ancient stone wall in need of repair like one would find in the old medieval days, but this one was older and very strange.

In front of her was a large wood and stone building that seemed to extend out of sight above her. Ledges every thirty or forty feet indicated an entrance inside if one could reach the platforms. Directly in front of her was a large oak door blocking her path, she had an overwhelming urge to enter the building.

No longer intimidated she smashed the door down with her foot. She was surprised her foot didn't go through. At the same time, she felt the flood of power. She could have some effect on this 'Being'.

Feeling better, she entered the passageway, but this was blocked with another door bigger than the last one. Not stopping, she smashed it in and walked through.

The next door had a guard blocking it. A large man dressed in a partially clad animal skin that enhanced his massive hairy chest. He drew his long blade and started toward her. Threatening, he attempted to frighten her.

At first successful she backed until she was against the wall. She watched the huge blade going up over her head. The outside light sparkled off the polished steel focusing her attention to the blades' cutting edge.

"She was going to die! She was going to die!" Through the corner of her eye she saw a similar blade hanging on the wall slightly to her right. A quick fake to left brought the blade down just missing her left shoulder, but now she had the one off the wall. Bringing it down hard on her antagonist, she allowed the blade to work, splitting his big hairy chest. "Here! Try this on!" She shouted.

He disappeared. Others took his place. These were bigger, and more massive. She kept swinging, taking out one, then another until the passage way was clear.

"Do you have any more?" She yelled at the 'Being' in her head. Keeping her sword in hand, she moved down the hall ready to take on another. Her confidence was soaring.

She sensed something with a musky decay smell coming from the room ahead. Swinging the door open, she found herself in an ancient torture chamber. Moving slowly, she noticed a man lying on a stretching rack on the far side of the dungeon. Seeing her, he screamed in pain, begging for release.

"Please help me before she tightens it again."

Ignoring him, she walked past, smashing the door in beside him with her sword. The man, thinking the swing was meant for him, stopped his pleas.

Walking into the hall, she noticed the depressed feeling became more intense. Decay upon decay was everywhere in body and soul. It felt like she was walking through the rubbish in someone's mind that has been accumulating over thousands or maybe millions of years. It was more of an emotion then something she could see.

People's faces began coming out of the walls. They were beautiful one second, then turned to ugly distorted pieces of flesh. When they came sweeping toward her, a deep cord of fear surfaced. She swung the sword hard knocking them out of the air. Successful at first, but each contact dissolved part of the sword until only her fists were left. Not hesitating, she hit one then another, but now her fists were covered with rotting flesh.

Becoming angry, she hit a few more flying faces, and began running. Enough of this! She didn't like the rotting flesh on her hands! She didn't like this tunnel! Kicking in harder, she picked up speed. The tunnel began to take on a new look. Smooth soft material replaced the old rough wood. Rapidly it was becoming like the hallways one would find on Star Base Twelve. It appeared clean with a light greenish color. Her hands cleared up. The rotting flesh disappeared.

She felt better. Maybe she did have some control. The tunnel wasn't straight. She found herself ducking protruding structural pieces. More, she wasn't running! Her feet no longer touched the floor. Moving faster, she came closer to the protrusions. She placed her hands in front of her and used her body to change directions with the tunnel. She sensed something ahead. It appeared to be a large compartment of sorts. It was dark except for a bright object in the middle of it. She turned toward it. Closer, the object was a young woman smiling at her. It was Judy! "What?" She asked. "How did you know about her?" Her anger swelled. It wasn't Judy! The 'Being' was using her.

Aiming for the figure with her fist doubled and extended, she struck it square on, nothing, it evaporated except for a sticky substance. She was covered with it. More, it was burning her!

She tried to rub it off, but she ended up making it worse. Her skin was on fire! She was a human torch flying through the dark green tunnel screaming until the blackness took her away.

She woke up cold muttering to herself. "I am Captain Ana Mc Clure of the Starship Neoann! I am Captain Ana Mc Clure of the Starship Neoann!" She said it over and over trying to reach reality. She was exhausted emotionally and physically. She couldn't take more!

She felt cold. Sitting up, she opened her eyes to a heavy fog bank. She couldn't see, but her hands told her she was sitting on ice. Knowing this would not last, she shouted, "What's next you fiend?"

Becoming colder, already her uniform, or what was left of it, was soaked from the damp air. This made her colder. She checked her arms. The sticky material had left its mark. She could feel the puffy welts going the length of them. She still hurt, but the cold helped to take some of the sting out.

She could not understand why the sudden turn of kindness until she began to feel colder. Her mind already knew it wouldn't be long before the deep penetrating cold reached her bones causing her more pain. "Perhaps I will freeze to death. If only I could, then it would be over."

She could hear her teeth chattering. She closed her mouth tighter to stop them, but it only transferred the shaking to her body. Finally opting for the clicking, she opened her mouth, and dropped her head. She wrapped her arms tighter around her legs seeking the remaining warmth from her body.

She had to think. She must take advantage of the time, or she will never get out of this hell. Yes, she meant hell! Every definition she has ever heard fitted this place. One didn't die here. She knew, she should have long ago. One only suffered with every fiber of their 'Being'. "Pain!" Her mind yelled. Excruciating pain until one could suffer no more. Then she had a moment to recover before she was thrown into the next torture. Already the freezing wind was cutting through her skin. How long before the pain in her bones reached her brain? "Think! I have to think!"

"Wind!" She felt wind? Lifting her head, the fog bank had lifted to reveal a barren landscape of ice. The glare forced her to close her eyes knowing she could be blind in seconds.

She didn't like this, not seeing. She was falling into the whirling black hole. Something was attacking her. She could not breathe. It was squeezing her heart! The pain! She heard Judy's screams. No! She wouldn't let them know about her dream! Pushing it further inside, she kept it away from the probing box. "Why did I think that? I like the darkness. In fact, I will sit here until things change," she thought. "It will! I know it will."

The wind velocity increased cutting into the tender skin on her face. She dropped her head into her lap attempting to cover herself with her freezing arms again. She felt the cold numbing her exposed skin. Dark, it was meant for warmer climates.

Maybe this was her punishment for using it to get her command. She passed over others older who lacked her gender and color. She could still see the look in Craine's eyes. He knew she didn't belong. Why was she thinking this? She has proven herself repeatedly. "Henderson accepts me!" She said, softer, "Henderson accepts me..."

Her mind drifted, she was remembering Lieutenant Colley. She didn't want to hurt him. She told him, but he forced her. Tears were developing.

"Well look at me now!" She said. "Oh God! Look at me now! Bubbling in my tears over things, I can no longer control."

Maybe this was all a nightmare. She could still be in her suit floating in the darkness, and her mind has snapped. The cold she felt was in her mind. "Maybe my frozen hair isn't real," she said aloud. Reaching behind her head, she took a handful, bent it and heard the slight snap. She felt the clump fall free. "No! No! Not my hair!" She shouted. The one part of her body she was the proudest of. Now, it was a freakish mess.

Her mind flooded with scenes of her combing her long soft curls extending down her back. Her hair was the best thing she inherited from her grandfather. He was curly, red head, and white. He loved her grandmother enough to give up his family. A whirlwind courtship and they were married within the week. Then, all he knew was black. "Her black! Her blackness!" She yelled.

Letting her mind fill with his memory made the pain less,

but something else was forcing its way in. She tried to push it out, but she couldn't. Her survival instinct demanded she focus in.

It was staring at her! Yes, it…It was coming towards her! She could feel it! Not daring to look she kept her eyes closed praying it would go away. Again, on the wind she heard a grunting noise. "It…It's coming toward her," she said under her breath. "Whatever it is, it knows I am here!" She couldn't move. She wanted to open her eyes, but she didn't dare.

"No! No! I must control my fear!" It…It was standing in front of her. Its huge body blocked the wind! She felt its hot smelly breath flowing over her. The foul stench actually felt good on her frozen arms.

Suddenly it roared! Feeling herself about to be engulfed, she lifted her head, and looked into the large jagged teeth coming down. She screamed! She let every fiber in her 'Being' scream! Her fear dominated. All thoughts of control had vanished.

The beast, surprised by the outburst, backed off slightly. He became angry swatting her hard across the left shoulder with his huge paw. Its claws cut deep into her black flesh and sent her cascading into the dark tunnel screaming with pain. Her mind felt the oozing blood flowing down her arm.

It didn't matter. She was out of there moving to another torture. She had only seconds, but it seemed longer. "Think! I must think! My ship! Where is my ship in this nightmare?"

4 Possession

She kept her eyes closed. She didn't want to see the next terror, but it was already too late. She had arrived! It was quiet! "Too quiet!" She said softly. There was no wind. The temperature seemed bearable. "Where am I?"

She didn't dare open her eyes? She felt the confinement. Moving slightly, her sore shoulder contacted something hard. It sent pain racing through her body. It almost caused her to pass out. Gritting her teeth, she recovered. Slowly raising her other arm, she felt a covering of some sort.

Trying to turn, she felt more of the fabric. It was familiar! "Yes! Yes!" She yelled. "It's my suit!" Opening her eyes, she looked around quickly, but all she could see was the blackness. "No stars! No light! Maybe this isn't my suit," she thought.

No, feeling it more, she found the controls. "Yes, it's mine!" Feeling for the light pack switch, she flipped the outside light on. "Darkness! There's nothing but darkness." She turned it off.

She didn't like the reflection.

She felt a small lump of something push in the side of her suit and slip on by. It frightened her at first. She almost turned on the outside light, but she didn't. "I'm in the black 'Being'!" She said aloud.

"My oxygen," she thought, "I should check that! How long did I have?" Quickly she turned the internal light on. "Twelve minutes!" She said aloud. "Twelve minutes of life, then I will suffocate and die." She had already resigned herself to the fact. It didn't matter.

She started to turn the light off to conserve the battery. "This is silly," she thought. "I will be dead long before it gives out." Flipping on the outside switch, she flooded the darkness with light. It made her feel better. Her last twelve minutes would be without fear. She didn't like the darkness. Screaming, "You hear that Psych! I don't like the darkness!" Holding back her tears, softer, she said. "I don't like the darkness!"

Pulling herself together, she forced her emotions down. She began checking her suit. "That's it," she thought, "Think, the oxygen, yes, ten minutes now. I must keep busy." Next, she checked the thruster pack. "Maybe I can blast out of here," she reasoned. "Perhaps I can find a star constellation, but then what? And which way is that?" There were three hundred and sixty by three hundred and sixty degrees to choose from.

"Maybe my odds are better. Maybe any direction is good. I could be in a small circular dark portion of the field." With nothing to lose, she hit the thrusters.

She felt the acceleration on her back and moved her left shoulder some to ease the pain. She had no idea of her direction. She focused on the inside panel allowing the computer to work. She was surprised it did remembering it didn't before.

Eight minutes later the thrusters cut out. Normally the pack would last her a full day using small amounts and drifting, but she needed speed now. She felt the black mass slipping by. She was creating her own current. Either she was blasting her way further into the black mass, or she was heading out. Her shoulder felt better. The pressure was off, the pain dropped to a bearable level.

"The transponder!" The thought flashed through her head. She flipped the switch on. A useless gesture with only two minutes of oxygen, but it was something to do.

Then she saw them. A few stars at first, then more came into focus. She was drifting out! She was drifting out! She had only a minute left of oxygen, but she would die with the stars.

Suddenly the communicator blared. "Captain Mc Clure! Captain Mc Clure! Is that you?"

The loud sound sent her into shock a moment. She didn't expect this. Her head filled with fear. It was Henderson's voice.

"Captain Mc Clure, respond," he said. "Have you on tracking. We'll be there in two minutes."

Immediately she cut her oxygen off to conserve the precious gas. She relaxed her mind and tried to use less. "Maybe I should leave it off and die before they reach me," she said unaware the lack of oxygen was affecting her. "No, I will still be alive. They will still see me like this."

A new feeling emerged inside her head. "Like what? I am the Captain! They did what I said! I rule here!" Her confidence came back, and she flipped the switch to allow the oxygen in. "They are mine to do with as I pleased."

Something began to bother her. She couldn't put her finger on it. "Where were these thoughts coming from?" Suddenly realization took hold. "They're not mine!" She gasped. "Oh my God! There's somebody in my head!" A wave of fear swept through her. There was something alive in her, and she was taking it back to the ship.

She tried to raise her arm to open the value to her suit, but the 'Being' inside prevented her. "I'll stop you!"

"Captain Mu Clure! Respond! Captain Mc Clure we're opening the hatch, bringing you in." It was Henderson's voice.

Ana didn't hear him. She had lost consciousness. Her oxygen had run out. The shuttle doors opened. A long arm eased the spacesuit inside. Immediately the compartment was flooded with oxygen.

Mr. Henderson reached in, opened the suit, and gave the life-giving oxygen to his Captain.

Slowly she opened her eyes. She saw the sudden fear in Mr. Henderson. Yes, she liked the control, but why the fear? She felt someone in her head trying to push her aside and speak through her mouth. Tightening her lips, she said, "Leave…Leave me be…" Then she was pushed aside. She heard her mouth still talking. "Put us on the tractor beam, then make the ship ready to go in. We're…" She pushed back attempting to regain control. Pushing harder, a little more, she almost had it. "We're…" The voice tried to say.

Concentrating, she was gaining. The 'Being' was moving aside. "This is my body! Get out!" Suddenly she was free. She screamed this last thought at Henderson. "Get out!" She felt the heavy pressure in her head suddenly lift. A greenish mist floated off, but she could only see the hurt look in Henderson's eyes.

"Yes ma'am! Sorry! Maybe Parker can help you."

She nodded and fell back in the suit. At least she controlled her mind. She was going to respond to Henderson, but she didn't. She watched him leave. Free of the 'Being', she felt better. Now they could leave, but something was bothering her. Had she seen something drift toward Mr. Henderson?

Doctor Parker pushed his way in, and opened her suit, "Easy girl! You didn't need to bite his head off. You look like hell! What happened in there?"

"Later Parker!" She started to lift herself out of the suit, "Did you see…"

"No, you don't!" He said pushing her back in. "I'm checking that wound on your shoulder first!" He worked his way more into the compartment. "You'd think they'd make these things larger. Now, let's see what we have here." He ran his portable medical analyzer over her. "It seems to be mostly the shoulder. Deep cuts, like you've been in a fight with a polar bear."

"You're close, we'll talk later but help me out of here." She lifted herself up using the doctor's arm.

"The shape you're in, you ought to be in my infirmary for a few days!"

"No time! I need another uniform! I'm freezing! See if you can find me one." She pulled herself through the hatch. "I'm heading for the com. I can't let him take us inside!" Using the hand rails, she left Parker looking at her hard, and floated towards the front of the shuttle.

Mr. Henderson was working the controls taking them back to the ship. She pulled herself up beside him. "Sorry, Mr. Henderson, I didn't mean that back there. The stress, you know. I didn't think I would…"

He turned to faced her. "Think nothing of it. We'll be inside in six minutes."

His calm voice tipped her off first, but the greenish yellow hue in his eyes confirmed it. The 'Being' possessed him! "Belay that last order! We're not going into that black mass! I want full thrusters out of here!"

"Whatever for, ma'am? You're behaving very strangely. I think you need a few days in the psych tank."

"I don't need the tank, but I think it might do you some good." She reached for the shuttle's communication button. "This is your captain speaking…"

Mr. Henderson closed the communication. "I don't think you heard me. Until you're checked out, we can't trust your ability to command."

"What do you mean? I am the Captain here!"

"Was is the operative word here. Look, ma'am, you've been in that thing twenty-two hours with a twelve-hour oxygen pack. How you survived I don't know, but the lack of oxygen may have done severe damage to your mind affecting your ability to command. All I'm asking is a few days in the psych tank to check you out."

Doctor Parker with a uniform in one hand pulled himself in with the other. "Found this one, it could be a little large."

She turned to Parker. "Tell him I'm okay so I can get my ship out of here."

"What's going on here?"

"She needs to be debriefed!" Mr. Henderson replied. "She doesn't like it!"

"Hympt! I agree with the Lieutenant here! That's standard procedure," Parker said turning back to her. "You know that!"

"Yes! Yes, but not now!" She pleaded. "This black mass is dangerous. We need some distance. Look at him, Parker. His eyes…They're…"

Parker gave Mr. Henderson a quick look, and then stared back at her. "He seems all right. It's you I'm worried about."

The overhead speaker blared, "Bay doors are open."

Mr. Henderson nodded towards them, "You better strap in."

Ana, seeing she had no choice, quickly put on the loose-fitting uniform, and took her seat as the craft moved into the ship's shuttle bay. The magnetic locks took hold and the air walkway was attached. The doors opened, and on the other side was Judy.

She ran in and gave Ana a big hug. "I'm so glad you're alive," she cried.

Ana, responding, said, "Thank you, Judy. It's nice to see someone missed me." She gave Parker a curt stare.

"Hympt! Need to get that shoulder fixed! Then I want to know how you survived twenty-two hours on a twelve-hour pack."

Pulling herself free of Judy, she followed the doctor off the shuttle, but not before she gave one more command to Mr. Henderson. "Take this ship out of here, and I'll get in the psych tank for you."

Mr. Henderson smiled, "That's all we ask."

A few minutes later Ana was in the ship's infirmary. She was having her left shoulder drawn back together. Doctor Parker was taking great delight in her discomfort. She would not allow him to put her under.

"You don't feel that, do you?"

"You know I do!"

"Then let me give you some anesthesia."

"And put me out of action?" She asked, defying him. "No way! We're in an emergency situation here." She pulled her arm back when the laser licked her again.

"Then hold still," he commanded and continued to work in silence. Finishing, he asked, "What are we running from? No one seems to know, but you." His voice softened. "What happened in there, Ana?"

He used her first name breaking all codes. He wanted a personal answer. Could she trust him?

When she didn't answer, Parker continued. "We find this dark mass where nothing seems to penetrate, like it absorbs all energy, but not really. Our probes come up empty. You decide to check it out taking me and Mr. Henderson with you. We stop at the edge of the thing. You don a suit and enter it. No one can talk you out of it, but we manage to persuade you to accept our wire. We track you until the wire breaks. We lose you for twenty-two hours until you finally emerge just before your twelve-hour oxygen pack runs out. That's on record. It's all we have! I would like to complete the log?"

"Hell, Doctor! I mean really hell! You know, the place the religious centers want us to believe exists. Well, I'm here to tell you it does exist! It's here! It's inside that dark space."

She allowed this to sink in a moment and looked at him hard. Then she decided she needed to tell someone. "I went all the way through the black mass, Parker. Inside, I found an enormous energy field with every color you can think of. It seems the black cloud mass protects it or keeps it from escaping. I have not figured out which."

Parker didn't say anything. She continued, "I was feeling cramped in my suit, and found the field carried enough oxygen to breathe. Even more amazing than this, I found solid ground to walk on. Now, I know it was reading my mind, and producing these things."

Then Parker interrupted her. "It? What exactly is this it?"

"I don't know, God! The Devil! A force field for sure that can create whatever you wish or create your worst nightmares. I do know this, you don't die. I should have, but I didn't. It wanted my body. It put me through all kinds of tortures trying to force me out of it."

"You can get hurt! Your shoulder can testify to that."

Ana sat up and reached for her hair. "Yes, and more, you better chop off the rest of it."

The Doctor nodded, picked up his electro-surge, and made a clean cut. The tangled mess of hair fell to the floor.

"I got that burnt in the burning tunnels after I left the lava spewing volcano."

"Lava! Volcano! That means a solid planet!"

"Yes and no," she replied, "I don't know! It's more like how I perceived hell and that is what it made. The pain was real, and the damage done to me was real. The rest, well, it could have been my imagination."

"Then how did you get out?"

She stood up testing her legs. "I don't know? I just found myself in my spacesuit. I must have gotten into it by myself, or…Or I never got out of it to start with, and this was all a dream." She looked up at Parker, continuing, "I don't know!"

"Maybe, but the oxygen packs were good for twelve hours. You were in for twenty-two. We didn't expect to find you alive. You must have been breathing something besides your packs. I wouldn't be so quick to dismiss the possibility of being out of your suit."

"Then you believe me?" She was almost pleading, but his eyes said not yet.

"What else happened?"

"I told you! My worst nightmares became realized. I was burning in hell one minute, and then freezing the next."

"I think we better be getting you into the psych tank."

"Later, Doctor," she said pulling her uniform on. She flexed her arm and flinched at the pain.

"That is going to be sore for a while. I don't think you're in any condition to…"

Suddenly the ship shook hard like it had entered something solid.

She looked at Parker. Her face registered fear. She headed for the hatch. "He's taking us inside!"

"Just a sec!" He called after her, "I'm not finished!"

She was already in the hall.

In the lift her mind was racing. He was possessed! Oh my God, she thought. Who was going to believe her? Maybe she should not have told Parker.

The bridge hatch opened. She immediately looked at the screen. It was black! She glared at Mr. Henderson. "What happened?"

"Nothing, ma'am! We're in the black field!"

Startled, she saw the greenish orange in his eyes. "I told you to take us away from here!"

"Sorry, but we heard your debriefing. Either you're not fit to command, or we need to prove your story."

The lift opened again, Parker stepped out. Ana immediately whirled on him. "Parker?"

He shrugged his shoulders. "Procedure, ma'am, procedure, you have to admit being gone twenty-two hours with a twelve-hour oxygen pack is a bit unusual."

She turned back to Henderson. "It's too dangerous!" She yelled. "Now, get my ship out of here! We'll discuss my mental condition later."

Mr. Henderson standing higher on the platform, looked down at her, "No, ma'am, I am in charge. I say we continue."

"And get the whole crew affected! You heard what I went through!"

"The decision is made. Now, if you will take her below to her cabin Doctor Parker, I'll get us through this black muck, and see if there really is a magic land."

She already knew what he or it wanted. Her ship flashed in her mind. If he could prove there was nothing there except darkness, then he can prove she was unfit for command. How can she handle a starship if she were afraid of the dark and hallucinated? If they did break through, she knew the 'Being' would infect her whole crew.

Parker reached for her arm to take her back. "I think he is doing you a favor, ma'am. If we leave without proving your story, you'll be relieved of your command permanently!"

The 'Being' in Mr. Henderson smiled. It liked her small victory. "Listen to him," he said. "We are trying to help you."

Allowing the doctor to lead her, she kept looking back at the greenish glow in Mr. Henderson's eye until the lift hatch closed. His personality had changed. "Like…Like he was someone else," she thought. Closing her eyes, she felt the lift going down. She had to be careful. They could still be monitored.

Reaching her room, she pulled Parker inside and closed the hatch. "You've got to listen to me!" She pleaded.

Parker edged back toward the hatch. "I think we already have."

"No! You don't understand. I'm not sure if this is another nightmare or real, but I do know this. Our new captain may be possessed by that creature inside."

The doctor's eyes widen. Immediately he confirmed his earlier diagnosis. "Your psych tank results said you had trouble with total darkness. I think you…"

Ana interrupted him, shouting, "You know my psych test didn't show that!"

"Ah, but I..." He started to say.

She approached, looked him in the eyes. "This has all been a set up. Send her off into the darkness and watch her go crazy."

"No, not by me, I'm not part of that. My job is to protect this ship and its crew. I didn't tell you to go into that black field. That was your own idea. Probably a guilt thing," he said moving closer to her. "In fact, I believe you wanted us to find out about your fear."

"Then explain my shoulder and burnt hair," She said pointing to the burnt piece on the floor.

"Could have done it to yourself."

"The time Parker!" She shouted. "What about the time? Ten hours past oxygen burn out."

"Yes, that is puzzling," he said, rubbing his chin.

"There's more, I'm afraid I did it too."

Parker looked at her close thinking now he would get the truth. His hand moved to press his communicator.

"No, not this time!" She took the device from his belt. "This is for your ears only." She waited for Parker to settle down. She knew he didn't like losing control, but he listened. "I…I think we have an intruder on board," she said in a quiet voice.

"Intruder?" He shouted. He shook his head, thinking she was losing her grip on reality.

"Yes," She continued, "I think I brought it on myself. It possesses Mr. Henderson."

"Mr. Henderson? Look, Ma'am, maybe…"

Interrupting him, she yelled, "Parker! Listen! This is important! Why are we going back inside this thing without probing it more? He's taking the whole ship, Parker!"

"But possession, that's hard to prove."

"Maybe not. That medical analyzer you use, does it measure brain waves?"

"Yes…Yes it does!"

"Could you analyze Mr. Henderson with it without him knowing?"

Parker nodded.

"Then here's the deal, if it shows an increase in energy then you will agree we have a problem. If not, then I'll submit to your Psych Tank."

Parker gave her a hard look. "If I get nothing, you'll go peacefully and sacrifice your career."

"What career, Parker? This thing can destroy us all. It allowed me to come back only to get the rest of you. Don't you see that?"

"Hympt! Maybe, then if it's negative, I see a very sick woman, agreed?"

"Yes! Yes! Whatever you say, but please hurry. I'll wait for you here."

Parker nodded, turned, and left. The door snapped shut

behind him. Ana began pacing. Her cabin was big by most standards, especially her crew, who shared their space. Of course, everything was in the walls, bed, sink, toilet, allowing her to walk without these things in her way. Finally, she pressed a few buttons on the wall control panel, out dropped her favorite chair and the bridge monitor. She could see what Mr. Henderson was doing, but she couldn't control it from here.

The blackness was thinning out. The screen showed the reddish orange colors and a space landing dock. The 'Being' had made a landing platform to receive the ship. It looked exactly like the one on Star Base Twelve except the background here was reddish orange instead of the normal backdrop of stars.

Didn't he see the danger? The 'Being' would read his mind, then produced his thoughts. "He's possessed!" She shouted at the screen. "He's possessed!"

Concentrating on the screen, she didn't notice Parker entering. "You can say that again!"

Whirling around, "You got it?"

"Like you said, it almost blew my analyzer apart!"

"He didn't see you do it, did he?"

"I…I don't think so, he…"

Suddenly over the speaker they heard Mr. Henderson's voice. "All hands! Doctor Parker has taken important information from the Bridge. Seek and detain! Seek and detain!"

"Nice going, Parker! I think it's time we go into hiding."

"You go ahead," he replied and sat in the chair. "I'll wait for them here. I'm not the cloak and dagger type."

"Have it your way," she said pressing the button that opened a sliding panel. She took out her weapons' belt. It carried a blaster, a wire glove, and a laser. She put it on and headed for the hatch. "See you later, Parker," she said going out, "Try and slow them down."

Moving down the hall, she decided her best chance was the lower decks. She needed to hide until she had time to think.

5 Fighting Back

The speakers blared again. "Captain Mc Clure has left her quarters! Apprehend! Apprehend!"

She fell into a side passage that led away from the gravity section and floated a moment. Where could she hide? They'll be using heat sensors.

Too late, two security men entered her space. She saw the determined look on their faces. She knew they didn't want to hurt her, but they would do their job. Pulling on the hand rails on each side of the chamber, they approached her. Slowly she backed up to the wider portion of the compartment forcing the two men to separate. Turning, she braced herself against the closed hatch behind her.

She waited until they were within two meters. Then bringing her feet up fast, she pushed off going between them. Both reached out, trying to grab her, but all they could do was watch. She flipped over and took their extended arms.

She jerked them hard toward her. The force reversed her direction ripping their hold from the bars. It sent them smashing into the open hatch at the other end. She stopped her momentum at the opposite door, opened it, and turned to see her two security men floating unconscious.

She felt sorry for them, but she couldn't let anyone stop her. She was the only one who understood the danger here. Quickly she opened the hatch. She dropped through a few more hatches until she found herself in the engine compartment. "Even if they figure out I'm here, it will take them time to find me."

She selected an air duct she knew eventually would lead her back up and climbed inside. She closed the hatch carefully trying hard not to attract the attention of the engine crew below. She could also see the ship's monitor on the far wall from here.

"All hands, liberty call! All hands, liberty call!" The loud speaker blared the message three more times before stopping, but the engine crew, already on the move, disappeared up the ladder.

On the screen in front of her, she saw her crew walking off the ship with Mr. Henderson in the lead. "He's taking everyone out. The fool! This thing is real!" Quickly sliding out of her hiding space, she brought the engines back on line. She started to head for the Bridge, when she heard soft footsteps coming down the ladder. Dropping back, she ducked behind the control panel and waited. The footsteps moved toward her. Even before she heard the voice, she knew who it was.

"Captain…Captain Mc Clure, I have come for you. This is your Yeoman, Judy. It is safe now. They are all gone."

Ana slowly moved around the control panel until she could see the back of Judy's head, yes, she carried a laser. She must be possessed. No one would use a laser weapon inside the ship.

She brought up her blaster, squeezed off a wide charge. It dropped her Yeoman immediately. Quickly she fell back behind the panel until the blaster's wave settled down. Looking back, she saw a light greenish orange mist lift from Judy's head and disappear through the bulkhead.

Like she thought, it could pass through the ship's skin, or anything it seemed remembering her spacesuit. Shifting her attention back to Judy, she moved up beside her. Kneeling, she checked her quickly, but there was no need for concern. The wide arc of the charge allowed only a small portion to stun her. She was already moving. "Sorry Judy, but sometimes it's for your own good."

Judy, staggering, worked her way to her feet. "How…How did I get here?"

"You were trying to kill me."

Tears began to fill her eyes. "I…I would never do that," she said in a soft voice.

"You would if that energy field possessed your body. Now, let's head for the Bridge, and retrieve our crew."

Judy allowed her to help the first few steps, then she pushed her away. "I'm okay, I'm okay. You have to believe me. I wouldn't kill you!"

"That Green 'Being' controlled your mind. It probably has more of the crew. Go to the infirmary and pick up one of Parker's scanners. Then stand by the main hatch. If you get a high reading on anyone, hit them with a charge from my blaster." She handed her the blaster. "It seems to force the 'Being' out."

"Do you want me to do everyone?"

"No, get some of them coming in to help, especially security. Now, get going!" She watched her move off a second. Then she started for the Bridge. She would get her crew back now that she knew how to fight the 'Being'.

Five minutes later "General Quarters" blared from the loud speakers outside. The crew knew it meant battle stations. Reacting out of years of discipline, they dropped everything and came running back to the ship.

When Ana reached the main hatch, she had a remote in her hand. She noticed Doctor Parker had control of his scanner, and security was standing by with their blasters. "Find any Parker?"

"They all seemed clear. I sent your Yeoman looking for Mr.

Henderson. He didn't show."

"You what?" She asked with an irritated voice. "She can't handle what's here!"

"Just what is here?"

"Later, Doctor! Let's get everyone on board. I want my ship out of here. Take a large orbit and wait twelve hours. If I'm not out with the two of them, fire two proton missiles into this thing."

"Where are you going?"

"After them!" She said holding up her remote. "Send the Alfa shuttle out. I have the ships course computations in its computer."

He nodded watching her disappear into the mist forming rapidly around them.

She stopped a second and yelled back. "Better set the transponder. I will need it to find my way back." Then the mist closed over her.

Parker quickly made his way to the Bridge. When he had everyone accounted for, he closed the hatch. He pressed a few buttons. The Alfa shuttle, with its transponder on, rumbled out of the middle of the ship and hung in the air. It had the ability to move over land or water. It could work in a gravity field by using its thrusters in a down direction.

When Parker saw the shuttle wasn't moving, he shook his head. "Should have waited for shuttle." Then he saw it move off. Smiling, "Good girl!"

Ana watched the shuttle emerge from the fog. In the distance she heard the ship's engines fire up. They became louder, then suddenly quiet when the ship entered the black morass. A feeling of desertion ran its course until she controlled it. She climbed into the shuttle and turned off the transponder. She opened the infrared screen.

Immediately she saw two images. The closer one had to be her Yeoman. Moving that direction, she left the fog bank. She found herself moving across a large ice field. The thrusters worked beautifully. She maneuvered over the smooth surface easily handling the wind. She saw Judy curled up in the middle of a large smooth area. She appeared unconscious.

The large beast that had attacked Ana before started to take a swipe at the unconscious girl. It stopped when it heard the shuttle's thrusters passing over. Frightened, it turned and moved on across the ice not waiting for a return encounter.

Ana quickly landed the shuttle, dropped the hatch, and ran to Judy. Dropping to one knee, she rolled her over to check her breathing.

Judy looked up, tried to open her eyes, "Sorry, I botched things up again."

"Sh…Sh. time to be sorry later. Let me get you inside." Easily carrying her, she had her in the shuttle. Strapping her in, she lifted off. Glancing back, she continued, "Sorry I don't have time to help you more, but I think our Mr. Henderson is doing a lot worse. I can barely pick him up on the screen."

The view screen suddenly went dark. She switched to automatic pilot allowing the computer to steer the craft through the rapidly closing tunnel. She didn't dare rely on her senses. The shuttle took a few bumps, but there was no serious damage.

Ana slowed the craft. They were approaching Mr. Henderson. The tunnel ended by opening inside the walled city. The infrared slowed Mr. Henderson loud and clear, but the other so-called humans, the drags of the earth, came up blank. This meant they were not real. "Yes, they could hurt, or was it her mind that caused the pain?" She asked herself. "Was she reacting to the event even to the extent of creating the deep cuts on her shoulder?"

Remembering when she became angry, she easily smashed their weapons and their bodies. Yes, these were emotional 'Beings' that could hurt you, if you allowed them to.

She saw Mr. Henderson tied to a cross on the third platform of the building she had entered earlier. She was in a square of sorts. All types of misshaped people milled around carrying lighted torches. They were looking for a place to throw them. "There must be close to thirty people," she said aloud. "Yes, our Mr. Henderson has quite an imagination."

Bringing the craft in low, she allowed the thrusters to work. It scattered the mob into hiding. Before leaving, they threw their torches into the sticks piled around Mr. Henderson's legs. The sticks immediately caught fire. It took a few more passes before she had scattered the sticks enough to place Mr. Henderson out of danger.

She started to put the craft down when the platform raised a hundred feet. The flaming sticks fell from the platform toward the shuttle. Quickly the flames intensified into a burning inferno. It sort of hung in the air protecting the platform.

She needed to hurry. Real or not Mr. Henderson was still in danger. Keeping the thruster on low, she looked back at Judy. "How are you doing?"

"Better."

"Can you function?"

"Yes."

"Then come up here and take this craft up to Mr. Henderson."

Judy stumbled forward. She looked at the viewer. A huge wall of flames was descending on the shuttle. "You…You're going out there?"

"Yes, and you're going with the shuttle. I'll clear a path for you."

"But why? The shuttle can…"

"I need to prove something," she said placing the remote in

her belt. She opened the upper hatch. "Close this after me but stay close. I may be coming back fast!"

Climbing up on top of the shuttle, she picked up a flaming stick that had fallen. Then into her wrist communicator, she said, "Okay, Judy, take us up." The shuttle began to ascend slowly. Ana felt the heat building. She prayed she had guessed right.

She shouted at the approaching fire storm. "Okay, that's enough! I don't believe in your fake fire! I don't believe you can burn me!" Ana heard a voice in her head.

It was the entity. "I burned you before. This time I will destroy you."

A huge mass of burning sticks began falling out of the cloud of fire. Using the stick in her hands, Ana started swinging knocking away the burning flames. At first frightened she moved the stick hard against her opponent. Though, after the initial surprise wore off, she dropped the stick. Then lifting her arms to protect her head, she allowed the flaming wood to fall. She easily knocked them away. Turning back toward the shuttles' outside camera, she waved her arm to let the horror-stricken Judy inside know to take them up.

Judy, following orders, took the shuttle up. She watched her Captain step off the shuttle and walk onto the platform. She entered the inferno! Judy could not believe her eyes. Seemingly Ana was not impressed with the heat she was picking up on her sensors.

Alarms on the shuttle were telling her the outer skin had reached its melting point. She had to take the craft back down out of the flames. Putting the shuttle in reverse, she left Captain Mc Clure to her fate in the flames of hell.

It didn't seem to do her any good. The alarms continued to ring in the shuttle. The screens showed immense flames scorching the outer hull. Over the shuttle's speakers she heard Captain Mc Clure's voice.

"Laury! Judy Laury! Turn on the transponder and put the shuttle on automatic! Then get away from the screen, strap yourself in. Do it now! That is an order!"

Judy allowed her left hand to do what she was told, but her mind was paralyzed otherwise. She could not take her eyes off the screen, nor could she understand how her Captain could take such heat.

Outside, Ana stood on the edge of the rocky platform ignoring the flames intensifying around her body. She had the shuttle slowly coming back up, but she seemed not to be aware of its blinking red lights. She brought the shuttle to a rest on the edge of the platform.

The screams of Mr. Henderson caused her to turn back. The barrier of flames was approaching him. If the 'Being' couldn't intimidate her, it would attack him. She knew the 'Being' wouldn't allow him to die. It still needed his body to operate the ship, but she was expendable.

No, the 'Being' was using him, trying to force her to accept his fear. If she did then all would be lost. There would be no rescuing her at the last second by taking her into the darkness this time. Without hesitating, she leaped into the flaming inferno.

The flames intensified. She could feel her skin wanting to ignite. She closed her mind off. Keeping it blank, she raced toward Mr. Henderson. A single thought would allow the flames to consume her. The inferno followed her until she reached Mr. Henderson. His screams filled her ears until suddenly the flames were gone. It left Mr. Henderson slumped over on his wooden cross unconscious.

She could smell his burnt clothing and hair. He looked bad! His body was filled with cuts and bruises. His legs, God, his legs, someone had cut the muscles to the bone!

Reaching down, Ana shook him hard. "Mr. Henderson!" She shouted, "Mr. Henderson!"

Slowly Mr. Henderson responded. He began mumbling. "No more! Please no more!"

She checked his eyes. The dark greenish yellow was gone. The 'Being' no longer possessed his body. Working her laser, she quickly began cutting his bindings. Done, Mr. Henderson fell towards her. "Best we get you out of here, Mr. Henderson."

Mr. Henderson began to move. "Where…Where are we?"

"Inside a living 'Being', but we can discuss that later."

Pulling him close, she tried to lift him, but he was too heavy. She needed help.

Suddenly the outside shuttle speaker blared. It was Judy shouting, "Fire's coming back! Fire's coming back!"

The fire, coming up over the structure, now sought its victims. It had already enclosed the back end of the shuttle. The flames moved rapidly up the stone structure around them. Ana could feel the intense heat. It threatened to consume then. Actually, the massive structure was dissolving into the flames. Only the top of the platform remained.

Ana, ignoring it, yelled into her wrist communicator. "Judy, I need a hand with Mr. Henderson. Get out here!"

"I can't! The fire, it's too hot!" She pleaded. "It…It'll burn us alive!"

"Wrap something around your eyes, and move it," she said in commanding voice. "I need only your legs. It seems they have cut Mr. Henderson's."

"Yes ma'am!"

A few seconds later Judy descended from the shuttle with part of a uniform tied around her eyes. "Please…I'll…I'll burn," she pleaded.

"No, you won't! I'm out here! Remember that! I'm out here with Mr. Henderson. Follow my voice!"

Judy stumbled towards her. "How come we're not

burning?"

"Because I don't want us to. Keep coming!"

Judy extended her arms feeling for them. Finally, she had Mr. Henderson's uniform.

"That's it," Ana said, "Now take his right arm."

The huge building was gone, yet they were standing on something solid. The flames quickly closed in creating a barrier between them and the shuttle. All they could see were the flames around them.

Mr. Henderson closed his eyes allowing the two women to drag him. He didn't care anymore. His skin, about to ignite, sent pain through his body. It was all he can do to remain conscious and help them. Maybe the fire would put an end to his pain, he thought. Then they could leave him.

Ana knew more. The shuttle may be gone. It could have fallen through the platform, or whatever they were walking on. She didn't dare let these thoughts surface. She knew this would be the reality. Instead, she concentrated on the shuttle being ten meters away. She shouted at Judy. "Pull him! I want him inside that shuttle!"

Judy, obedient, dug her feet in following her lead. "It too hot! We're going to burst into flames! I know we are!"

"No, we're not!" Ana yelled back. "The fire can't hurt you, only your mind can! You hear me Mr. Henderson! Get your mind right! Think cool breezes!"

"You…You have to be crazy! I can't…"

"You want to die here?"

"No!"

"Then do it! Do it now! You too Judy! Think ice! Feel how cool it is!"

Judy stood straighter. "It is cooler. I don't feel the fire!" She reached up and pulled off her blindfold. "Look, the fire's gone! There's ice everywhere!"

The fire had disappeared. In its place were three inches of ice. They were in the courtyard at the base of the huge stone structure. The shuttle, covered with ice, was five meters in front of them.

Mr. Henderson smiled, "Did you have to say ice?"

"We can make it fire again."

Mr. Henderson, doing better, tried to move his legs, "I don't believe this! They're working!"

"You better believe it, or you won't be leaving here. This place works on your emotions. If you feel fear, it produces it in all of its dimensions. Pain, love, whatever, you have to guard your emotions."

Reaching the shuttle, Mr. Henderson began chipping at the ice over the hatch. "I wonder what the love emotion is like in this place."

"Just keep thinking ice, Mr. Henderson!" Ana felt another presence behind her. Whirling, she saw a huge man with a large sword about to cut her in half. Behind him the people were coming out of their hiding.

Angry, she threw herself at him. "I'm tired of these games!" She shouted.

Her sudden attack sent him reeling backwards into the forming crowd. Ana pulled herself up and watched the crowd approach. "If more of you would like to get hurt just keep coming."

The crowd hesitated while the big man regained his feet. Slowly he lifted his weapon high over his head.

Ana closed her eyes and concentrated. Her body began to shake. She could feel her throat going dry. A huge dark purple energy field began to flood her mind. She didn't expect or seek this. It didn't frighten her. Instead, she felt invincible. The field seemed to be protecting her. Regaining control, she slowly opened her eyes. A dark purple cloud of energy hung over the courtyard. The crowd was gone, and so was the ice. Only the shuttle and the three of them remained.

Turning, she saw Mr. Henderson and Judy wide eyed looking at her. "What's wrong with you two? I just reverse what this thing has been doing to us. You created the ice. I thought I would try the dark cloud. I guess it worked."

Mr. Henderson was not doing well, boarded the shuttle, "If it's all the same to you, I've had enough!"

After helping him inside, Ana strapped him in beside Judy. "Yes, I think it is time! The big dark mass outside hasn't shown his hand yet. Maybe we shouldn't be in all that big of a hurry to take him on."

Judy, adjusting herself, said, "I'm with Mr. Henderson. You act as though this thing is alive!"

"Both are, what we have seen so far has been the weaker sensitive side. Out there you'll find strength and power."

Judy started to tear. "You mean he may not let us go?"

"Only if he thinks it's best for the sensitive 'being'."

Mr. Henderson mumbled softly, "I'm for giving him a run."

"Good, I'm glad you both feel that way, cause that's what I had in mind." She pushed the thrusters forward and turned the craft around. She started back to the coordinates where the spaceship had entered the black mass. She wanted to follow it out to keep her computer accurate. Not that it really mattered. The mass would change things. She had learned that!

The spaceport was gone. She knew it would be, but her little piece of heaven was back. Tempting, she remembered how it used to be years ago. She made a wide sweep, circled it once, then headed straight for the darkness.

Judy looked up at the screen. "It looks nice. Your home

isn't it? I can see why you liked it."

"Yes, I could have stayed there the rest of my life, but I didn't have enough sense to."

"No matter how the cage looks, it is still a cage," Mr. Henderson mumbled before he lost consciousness.

She nodded giving Mr. Henderson a quick glance. She didn't like his condition, but her attention was forced back to the black mass flowing over the craft. Flipping the automatic switch, she would let the computer take them out.

Suddenly they were struck from the side. The craft started to roll. Ana, taking back the control, turned the thrusters slightly, and gradually straightened the craft out. "That's it for the computer. It's all new territory from here."

They hit an upward current that almost sheared the craft. Ana barely managed this when the craft suddenly picked up speed. "Both of you into spacesuits and bring me one!" She yelled over her shoulder, "Check the thruster packs."

Judy released her belt. She pulled herself back to the lockers. "Plenty of suits, but only one thruster pack."

"Set it out! Then help Mr. Henderson into his suit. I'm not sure how long this craft can take this punishment."

Another rippling wave moved through the metal skin loosening several seams.

"Move it, Judy!" Ana shouted. She pushed the automatic

button, turned and pulled herself back to help.

Henderson, with a blank stare on his face, was not doing well, but he followed directions. It allowed them to ease him into his suit.

Another rippling wave took out the engines. The Blackness now had control of the shuttle.

Ana had the thruster in place and zipped up her suit. "That's it! Abandon ship! We'll have to use the thruster." Pulling a line from the locker, she connected the three of them. Then checking Mr. Henderson to be sure his oxygen was working, she pushed him out the hatch. He immediately disappeared into the black quicksand. Only the attached line was visible.

Judy turned, hesitated, "I can't see him! I can't see him!"

"That's why the line!" Ana yelled. "Now move it!" She gave her a shove and followed her. In seconds she was alone. She couldn't even see the line to Judy. She felt something pulling her. Then groping fingers pushed into her suit. It was Judy looking for her.

Switching her interior light on, she placed their face plates together. She could see Judy was frightened. Her eyes flowed with tears. "Easy girl!" She said in a soft voice. "I'm here! Now, let me work around you. I want Mr. Henderson here too!"

Working herself by Judy, she found the line to Mr. Henderson. Pulling, she had them together. Quickly checking his head plate, she tried to see his face, but his interior light was off. The man wasn't doing well. "Mr. Henderson! Mr. Henderson! Can you hear me? Turn your interior light on!" He didn't respond.

Holding him, she moved back to Judy, and tied him to her back. Then placing Judy's suit in front of her, she tied herself in. Only by placing their face plates together could they communicate. Judy was already clinging to her like a child to its mother with her legs and arms extending around her.

Bringing her arms to her side, Ana worked her thruster. She started them moving through the black morass. Not sure of her direction she went by feel and instinct. She knew she had to conserve her fuel. This was going to take a while.

Judy, leaving her light on, laid her head against the front of her head plate. Ana thought about telling her to turn it off to conserve the power pack, but then her oxygen would run out long before it did.

They crossed three more currents. Being small, the rippling effect didn't produce any shearing forces. Using her thruster, she managed all three easily. Finally, down to two hours of oxygen and one minute of power, she decided to give a thirty-second blast to attempt a break out.

Pushing the thruster button, she felt her spine pinching against her suit. In thirty seconds the power was off, and they drifted. They would go another hour before she would give the thruster another fifteen seconds. She would save the last bit of fuel for the last hour.

Suddenly the blackness was gone. The space was alive with stars! She looked around quickly. They were out! Tapping on the head plate, she woke up Judy. "We're out! We're out!"

Judy lifted her head, smiled, "Where's the ship?"

"Turn your transponder on! They can't be far!" She already had hers going. Adjusting the thruster, she gave it another five-second burn to put them in orbit around the black mass. She knew the ship could be on the opposite side hidden from their transponders.

With thirty minutes of oxygen left they heard Doctor Parkers voice. "Good to see you made it out, but where's the shuttle?"

Ana, smiling, said, "Lost it inside."

"I think you have a thing for spacesuits."

"Don't push it, Parker! We're in no mood. It was good the ship was on this side."

"It's not!"

"Then how…"

Interrupting, "I'm in Bravo Shuttle. I've been waiting for you. I guessed you might come out on this side."

"We've got thirty minutes of oxygen. How long before you get here?"

"Be there in two. How's everyone doing?"

"Judy's fine, Mr. Henderson, I don't know. He's hurting, but more mental than physical. He's catatonic."

"Hmm, okay, I'll bring him in first. You know the locks are small."

"No, take Judy first, she can help you with him. His legs are not working well. He has deep cuts, possibly to the bone."

"Bleeding?"

"He wasn't when I last checked." She could see the shuttle approaching. "Have you in sight now, Parker."

Two hours later they were on the ship. Mr. Henderson was in the ship's medical center being worked on by Doctor Parker. Judy occupied the bed across the way.

Captain Mc Clure, on the Bridge, was debating the best course of action against the dark mass outside. She had already sent a message to Star Base Twelve. Now she waited for a decision. She had the entire mass on the screen, but she kept her distance. Her mind began clicking through her weapon systems. She was trying to decide which one would do the most damage, when the speaker came alive.

"Captain! Captain Mc Clure!"

She reached over and pushed the communication button, "Yes Parker!"

"You better come down here. We have visitors."

"Visitors!" She knew what that met. She reached for her weapons' belt and pushed the communication button. "Security! Intruders! Medical section! Take no action until I get there!"

A few minutes later she entered the infirmary to see two fields of energy hovering a meter off the deck. One was a greenish yellow glowing mass. She had met that one before. The other, a dull black round mass, was from the dark strength side. The danger lay with this one.

Ana motioned to the two security guards outside. "No one approach them!"

Parker looked at her, "Didn't have any intention of doing so."

"Have they been threatening?"

"Not yet! I think they've been waiting for you."

Immediately the brighter field moved toward Judy, and the dark mass moved toward Mr. Henderson.

Ana drew her blaster, but they had already entered the bodies. She pointed her blaster at Mr. Henderson, but Doctor Parker stepped in front of her.

"You'll kill him with that blaster. His body can't take another jolt!"

"You think that black mass won't?"

"I don't know, but he can't tolerate another shock to his

system."

"Okay, Parker, we'll see what they want." She turned her blaster toward Judy. "She can take it! Speak up, or I'll blast you out of there!"

Judy's body adjusted, and slowly her eyes opened. The greenish yellow glint was evident. She looked around the room slowly. "It's been hard adjusting to your confinement. What you see through is interesting, but why only one direction?" The sensitive being asked.

"To help in our concentration they tell us," Ana replied, "Now get to the point!"

Actually the 'Being' was sending her emotions through Judy's mind. Then by using Judy's vocabulary, her voice emerged. "We thought we would become your God, but it appears you no longer need one."

"I didn't know God enjoyed making people suffer," Ana said with anger in her voice.

"We had no idea you would resist our control over you."

"If that's your best effort in the God business, then I think it best you moved off."

There was a moment of silence. The 'Being' in Judy closed her eyes and remained in Judy's body.

Ana thought she had waited long enough. "I said move off!" She brought up her blaster.

Mr. Henderson's body raised itself to a sitting position, turned toward Ana. A deep voice erupted from his throat. "She is afraid you are going to destroy us."

"And you?"

"The probability exists, but in the end, we may be your salvation."

Ana, not quite understanding what was being said, bluffed to hold the initiative. "You will not be allowed to approach closer. Even now my superiors are contemplating your destruction."

The 'Being' in Mr. Henderson began to laugh. He looked at Judy. "She doesn't understand! She doesn't understand!"

The one in Judy opened her eyes, smiled, "This one may be blinded, or they have destroyed their creator."

"Then we shall be its replacement."

Ana, trying for control, "I can see the spiritual centers working you two over. I think you'll find we have our God, and he's a very jealous one."

The one in Henderson became irritated. "Must we talk to these shielded ones who have so little knowledge?"

"Maybe it would help if you gave us some background on yourself. Like where you came from? Are there others like you? How did you manage to get into our system? Then, and only then you might be allowed to bloom."

Mr. Henderson swung his feet off the table standing. His eyes saying, he realized the gravity of what Ana said.

But the one in Judy did not catch the phrase 'bloom,' and shouted out, "We will tell you nothing! Perhaps I will set this one on fire and let her burn before your eyes."

Ana whirled and raised her blaster, when the one in Mr. Henderson's body spoke. "Hold! I said hold! I don't mean you, ma'am! I mean the one with the foolish thoughts."

Ana slowly turned back to him, "Do you control her?"

"Yes, I will make her behave. You must forgive her. She is not completed yet. She does not know how to control her emotions as I am sure you have found out."

"And I suppose you're the one of ice who operates without emotions."

"Yes, until I am completed."

"That's yet to be seen, isn't it?"

"As you say, ma'am."

"If you have a message, deliver it!" She looked at Parker who has been staring at the three of them. "Parker! Parker! Has the video been going?"

Doctor Parker snapped himself out of his trance and flipped a switch. "It's going now."

Ana turned back. "You've just had one break. My superiors

won't know how nasty you've been. Now, we'll hear where you came from."

"So, you desire to know of our heritage," Henderson's body began walking back and forth.

Parker started to resist him but stopped when he saw the deep cuts on Henderson's legs heal. Amazed, he stepped back.

The 'Being' in Henderson looked at Parker. "Hympt! You do impress easy!"

"I don't mister! Get on with it!"

"As you say, ma'am," The 'Being' knew where the power laid and directed his attention back to her. "Yours' is not the first successful completion. There have been others."

"You're from one of these?"

"Yes, and so was the one who gave birth to you. We were of the same 'Being'. Both sent adrift as pods. She has flowered. We haven't!"

"And where is this other 'Being' who creates pods, and then sends them out into the darkness?"

"The Greater Part no longer exists. The pods, floating free, are all that is left of him."

"How large was he in comparison to our system?"

Mr. Henderson laughed, "You would be but a twinkle in his

mass."

"Then what could possible destroy something that large?"

"Himself," he replied, "The black whirling holes consume all energy without leaving a residue. Instead of creating, it does the opposite."

"And he produced such a thing? Why?"

"To balance himself at first," the 'Being' inside Mr. Henderson said. "The creative part of him was getting out of hand, going too fast, leaving unfinished residue behind. His wave became clogged with debris. So, he produced the black holes to clean himself up."

"That's when he lost control of the black holes?"

"No, he controlled them right up to the end. He delayed his destruction until his pods were completed."

"Why?"

"To start over, he could no longer control what he was, or did he want to. He simply was too big. There was nothing new. The most exciting thing was his destruction. He took great pleasure in it."

"Then why the pods?"

"I said, to start over! He produced millions of them."

"Then why have we seen only you?"

"Because he also produced millions of pods containing his destructive machine. Whenever one of us bloomed, it would attract several destructive pods. Immediately one would bloom beside it and consume its energy."

"Then there has to be millions of whirling black holes around."

"Yes and no. Once the whirling black holes have bloomed, they must consume mass. The ones that consumed our creator became quite large, but in the end, they consumed themselves."

"If I'm getting this right, there are pods out there that can create and there are pods that can destroy."

"Yes, but you are the only one who has been successful after the bloom that we are aware of."

"You mean all the other millions have been consumed?"

"That, or they are in another part of the darkness, or they remain as pods looking for a safe place to bloom. All of this knowledge should be yours."

"It's not! Yours is the first pod we have explored. It appears we must check each encounter."

"You will allow us to bloom?" The 'Being' asked.

Ana closed her eyes. She felt a heavy presence dropping over her. Her body shook, and then a deep course voice came through her. Shocked, she found herself in a small portion of her head. The voice did not exclude her from hearing, nor did it seem to be threatening, but it wasn't her voice. "No! It will not be allowed! More must be learned."

The one in Judy protesting, "What does she know? We gave her what she wanted!"

Mr. Henderson shouted, "This is not her! Listen! Can't you feel his power? But you do ask a good question."

Ana, her voice remaining deep, asked, "You do not really know?"

"We know you bloomed. It appears you still retain your creator. Why do you need us?"

"For your knowledge," she said. "Once you bloom, it is lost! You will become a helpless 'Being' in the darkness until you learn to survive."

"If we decide not to cooperate?"

"We will cast you adrift, and let your fate be decided by your luck. Cooperate, and we will protect you through your critical stage." The voice left Ana. She could feel herself moving back into her body, and the heaviness fading out. She looked around quickly to be sure she still had control.

The one in Henderson continued to stare at her. "We did not know! We did not know! It has always been so obvious. That explains why they were so helpless when the destructors arrived. They did not know how to create. They did not even know they had to."

The one in Judy asked, "It's not going to let us, is it?"

"No, my dear, it will let us, but our chance of survival is a million to one. Let him protect us, and it will be assured."

Ana sensed the conversation needed to end. "I think that about covers it. Now, if you will move yourself out, it will be appreciated."

"Yes, at once! May we stay close?"

Ana, shaking her head, said, "No, you must move to the outer edge of our universe. We will not be having you exploited." The words sort of flowed out from deep inside. She continued to maintain control of her body, but she knew something else was putting these words in her mouth.

"As you say," the 'Being' replied.

Suddenly Henderson's body fell to the floor. Immediately Judy's body followed. The two 'Beings' had left.

Doctor Parker, in shock up to this point, had only partially heard the conversation. He understood none of it. Suddenly he became aware of his patients on the floor. He checked Mr. Henderson's vital signs first, "He's alive! The thing didn't kill him!"

Ana, letting Parker handle Mr. Henderson, checked Judy. Her limp body slowly regained consciousness. She was already coming around when Ana lifted her to a sitting position. "You're going to be all right. The 'Beings' have left for good."

Judy, still frightened, sought comfort in Ana's arms until Doctor Parker forced her to her feet. "Up! Up! Let's see if you can stand."

Mr. Henderson, already sitting on the table, was checking his legs where his wounds had healed. "Everything Parker! It healed everything!"

"Too bad he didn't stick around longer to show me how he did it. Some Captain I know of sure was in a hurry to get rid of him."

"They were strange 'Beings', Doctor. Maybe I should have told them to crawl around inside your head."

"Thanks, but no thanks! I see your point! How do you feel Judy?"

Judy shook herself, "Okay, I think."

"Good!" Parker said. "Cause both of you are heading for the psych tank. I'm going to see what those 'Beings' did to you."

Ana, starting back toward the Bridge, said. "Now that this is done, I've got a ship to run."

"Not so fast, Captain!" Parker said. "You'll be going in right after them."

"Me? I feel fine!"

"No buts! I heard something weird come out of you too. I

have it all on the video."

Ana stepped over to the monitor. She pushed some buttons, but only the first phase of the conversation came through. The part Ana spoke differently in wasn't there.

"Looks to me like you turned the machine off, Doctor. I don't recall any conversation, and the machine doesn't show anything. Maybe you were having a difficult time orienting. Could be you need some tank time yourself."

"Clever, Captain, but I know what I heard."

"Good! I'd keep it to myself. We would hate to have people probing your mind."

Suddenly the loud speaker blared interrupting the conversation. "The black mass is moving off! It's heading for the outer galaxies. You should see the speed. It's already off our sensors. It left our shuttle. We're maneuvering to pick it up."

Ana smiled, "I guess our little talk did some good."

Judy looked at Ana. She was still a bit shaken, "Do I have to?"

Ana gave her a big hug. "Yes Judy, we must check for permanent damage, but I'll be close by." Looking at Mr. Henderson, "You'll follow her. It'll give you time to fill in your log."

Mr. Henderson, with a tear coming to his eye, asked, "Permission to give the Captain a hug?"

Ana, smiling, said, "Yes!"

All three pulled each other closer while the doctor looked on. "Now that's cozy."

Some distance away moving rapidly through space, the two 'Beings' making up the pod were evaluating their encounter.

"Did we do well?" The sensitive being asked.

"Yes, our survival is assured," the strength side said, "The woman was a direct link."

"No wonder I was unable to destroy her mind. "Though the male was quite easy."

"Yes, we should be thankful it was allowed. We must take greater care in the future."

"The future will be ours! I can feel it!"

"And we will be his destruction," the strength side said, "Imagine how much bigger and stronger we will become if our bloom learns the knowledge of this one."

"Are you sure he will allow this?"

"He cannot help himself for the very same reason our creator destroyed himself." The black pod continued toward the outer edge of the universe with each feeling their bloom would be successful.

Prologue Two

The Dark Purple One:

The universe continued to whirl outward creating energy and becoming larger. The overall conscious was pleased. The success of his creation after passing through the focal point was progressing. Constantly evolving, he sent a new wrinkle through his body.

Of course, many things were attempted before they reached his focal point. Though once accepted, he allowed them to pass, and expand into the far reaches of his 'Being'. There to be expressed in every conceivable direction. He learned, then taking the best, he recycled it back through his plane before the focal point. He improved allowing the purity of the emotion to become a part of him.

No, he did not close off his source of creation. Not even the one who did not become part of him, the 'Creator of All Things,' the one who survived the melding process of the Black Pod. Even now he contemplated the need for her. She wanted control, and she wanted to survive. He wondered what emotion was stronger.

Already she controlled the plane before the focal point, and constantly tried to push through the point using every trick available to her. She knew where the point laid, but the strength of the 'Being' was too strong for her.

The overall conscious had other things on his mind. He was creating energy and grew at a phenomenal rate. He filled the darkness with life, but where did the energy come from? Did it come from the other side of the darkness?

Yes, he has learned how to draw this energy out and to create himself. The struggle caused enormous suffering, pain, and loss of souls, but he survived as recorded in the 'Creation of One'.

Now he wondered if this was part of a cycle. From the Black Pod he learned another 'Being', occupying quanta more darkness then himself, existed. Bored with creating, he destroyed himself with enormous black holes. These took his energy away leaving the darkness in its place. What intrigued him the most was the comment, "The 'Being' looked forward to it."

From his own experience he knew the cost of creating, the excitement, and then finally the completion. Why would he look forward to his destruction? Unless…Unless he was creating again. Not here, but somewhere else, maybe beyond the darkness.

The darkness could be a barrier of sorts with the black holes providing a channel except only in one direction. There was no return! Energy was created out of the darkness. Energy was reabsorbed into the darkness, thus completing a cycle. "Why?" He asked. What was on the other side of the darkness? Is 'All That He Is' only a portion of this cycle, yet to be absorbed into it? How far did the darkness extend? Was there another 'Being' moving through the darkness bigger or maybe smaller then him? Maybe they have tried to pierce the darkness only to find disaster, but then his predecessor found excitement in his passage.

Yes, he has taken a whirling black hole into his 'Being'. Controlling, he fed it enough to allow existence, but not enough to let it grow. Not yet anyway, he thought, not until he was ready to use it.

6 The Worm Hole

The Neoann Starship moved through space at standard speed towards the Alpha Twelve Star Base. Routine, Ana was taking a moment to relax. She leaned back in her favorite chair in the observation hall. She was tired. She has been pulling double shifts for the last two weeks while Mr. Henderson was in the psych tank. He pulled up clean. The results will go into his personnel file and be sent to Space Command. The repairs on the Alpha shuttle were completed. She placed it back into operation status.

Tomorrow they would reach Star Base twelve. She began to let her thoughts drift toward the base. She visualized the huge pools of water flowing over her body. This was an expensive luxury in space because of the enormous amount of recycling. It would cost her dear, but she didn't care. She allowed herself to drift under the water.

Suddenly she lost the image. Adrenalin filled her body. She

sat up straight with her senses alerted. She looked around slowly, but she did not see anything. The room was dark and empty except for the starlit sky on the dome.

Not sensing anyone in the room, she allowed her body to relax. Slowly she laid back on the floating chair. She must be really tired. She didn't understand why she felt threatened. She was safe here. That was one advantage of being on a spaceship. You didn't have to worry about some stranger attacking you. She trusted her crew with her life. Feeling safe, she allowed her mind to wonder. She began to absorb the masses of stars filling the dome above her. The Milky Way's billions of stars never seemed to change. They would always remain out of her reach. It would take thousands of lifetimes to reach even one of them. "Space time passes too slow," she thought. "Everything takes light years to complete. God must be very patient, or very bored."

"Neither!" A voice said.

"What?" Ana said startled. She sat up quickly looking around, "Who's here?" No one answered. She waited several minutes before she began to feel foolish and laid back. "Easy girl," she said to herself. "You talked Parker out of the psych tank once, but you won't do it a second time."

She adjusted her shoulders. "Must be overly tired," she thought. Yes, it was the confinement. Space fever some called it. Out here you could never be free. There was always the confinement. Even floating outside the ship, the spacesuit confined your movements, pressing in on your skin. "God, I need off this ship!" She said aloud. "One more day then I'll be on Alpha Twelve."

Looking up at the ceiling, everything seemed to be moving in slow motion. She knew it was the ship's movement causing the distortion.

"It can move faster." The voice replied.

This time she refused to sit up. She knew there was no one in the room. The voice had to be coming from her head. She remembered the deep voice coming through her when the Aliens were aboard. Maybe she should have taken some tank time. "Are you in my head?" She asked aloud.

"Yes, I am in your mind, and here physically too."

She quickly looked around, "Then, where are you?"

"About four feet above your head, but your senses are not perceiving me."

She turned toward the ceiling and the stars, but still she could not see anyone. "Hold it Charlie, or whatever your name is. I'm not into this! Better pick on another patsy."

"No, you have been selected," the voice said.

"I don't talk to spooks! God, what am I doing? Maybe I should see Parker!" She looked away and covered her eyes.

"Can we get on with this?"

"Not until I can see you," she raised her head slightly.

"Visually or inside your head?"

"Visually, Charlie! I'm not letting any spook in my head!" She could feel whatever it was smile.

"I am already in your head," the voice said. "Very well, we will make your experience more visual together. Please lay back on your platform."

Hesitant, but complying, she slowly laid back. "I not into any of this hypnosis gibberish." It's against the law, and I don't relish having my mind messed up."

"Will you please relax and concentrate on the bright star you call your sun," the voice said? The sun was small this far out. "Let your mind relax, breath deep. That's it! Now let the air out slowly and fall into the star. You need to become part of it."

She could feel herself drifting in. Fighting, she came back up some. "I told you no hypnosis! I am not going deeper in."

"It is not necessary. We don't need a dream state. We only want to increase your state of awareness."

She saw something drift across the star. A patch of mist, light orange in color, was coming back until it stopped slightly to the left of it. "Is that you?"

"Part of me, all that I care to show you at the present."

"I thought so! You're a spook!"

"No, I am the same as you except I do not possess a body as you do."

"You thinking about taking mine? It's been tried." Her mind recalled her encounter with the black pod.

"I do not acquire energy from others. Only gods, unable to produce their own energy do this."

"If you're not a god, then what are you, the Devil?"

"No, I am what exist before and after death. This knowledge is blocked of course while you are in physical focus."

"Handy I bet, so why the intrusion now?" She was aware of law against paranormal activities. Maybe she was being tested by some hidden-on board computer, but who would set it up. She was aware of some crews having moles aboard. They reported only to the High Achievers, or the priesthood of the religious order. They are the ones who sanction their deep space exploration. "Do I have one?" She asked herself. "Maybe I will play along and find out."

The entity continued to talk. "A great experiment is about to take place that will include you and your crew. I have been sent to educate you."

"That's great," she said. "A spook is going to give me lessons."

"I have a name."

"I'm game. What is it?"

She heard a musical tune, soft, two notes, a high one, and then a low one. "Well?"

"The musical notes!"

"No, you need a name, how about Charlie?"

"Whatever pleases you, now, can we get on with our lesson?"

She could tell he really didn't like the name Charlie, but because of this she stayed with it. "Okay, Charlie, I'm all yours."

"Very well."

The done ceiling slowly changed from a star background to one of a huge whirling black hole with an open center. Becoming more intense, the whole room turned into the whirling black mass. She was in the eye moving toward the very center where everything converged into one.

She remembered the black whirling mass in the black pod. Becoming nervous, "I think this is close enough, Charlie."

"It will be even closer later," Charlie replied. "You must pass through the eye."

"I'll be pulled apart. Then condensed to nothing, or become part of whatever else this thing sucks in."

"No, you will go through."

"How?"

"With tremendous speed you will past through into the other side, slow, reverse direction, and boomerang back through."

"Where will I get that much speed? What is going to keep our friend open until I return back through?"

"The black mass will be fed enormous amounts of energy. Much more than it can handle. It will cause the mass to increase in size, and the eye to open larger while it is adjusting."

The whirling image began to draw in surrounding stars, and then galaxies until the opening at the far end enlarged.

"That's when I'm supposed to pass through?"

"I think you understand."

"Okay, the speed, we can't go faster than the speed of light. So, when do you plan on doing this, a hundred billion years from now." She began to feel quite pleased with herself. This whirling black hole was hundreds if not thousands of light years away. Any school kid could calculate she will not get there in this lifetime.

"Yes, you will."

She forgot the spook was in her head. "How?"

The room began to change. The whirling black hole moved

off and more stars and galaxies filled the room. She could see in three dimensions. The visualization had depth, and emotion. Her mind understood the concept instantly. It all seemed so clear. A cord of energy threaded its way toward the black hole. The cord did not have definite borders. It was more of a flow of current where the energy moved in a circular motion around the cord as well. Closer inspection revealed a mass moving rapidly through this tube of energy.

"What is it?"

"An electromagnetic field of energy is the closest thing to compare it with."

"Who built it?"

"The overall conscious, or the 'Being' you are all a part of, allowed its construction. It is an electromagnetic gun that will increase your speed as you progress, similar to an electron moving through a coiled field."

She began to feel a heaviness descending over her. Yes, she was going to be in that tube of energy. "What are the probabilities of surviving?"

"Hard to say, this has never been done before."

"If I fail?"

"We believe it will be successful."

"You didn't answer my question."

"You will lose your soul, and everything that is you, will cease to be. Your memory may be retained, but your fabric will be absorbed."

"Charming."

"I wouldn't be all that concerned," he said in an even tone. "You have been absorbed many times already, but then your memory of the event was not retained. Failure is normal. Success, well, we try very hard, but we believe this will be successful"

"You're not part of this, are you?"

"Quite to the contrary, I am going with you."

"That's not what I meant!"

"No, I am not part of the overall conscious," Charlie replied. "I did contribute to his creation, but I never became part of him."

"How big is he?"

"All that you see, and much more you do not see. Actually, what you do see is his creative part. What he ultimately becomes, and the process in between is too dark for you to perceive in this focus."

"So, what are we doing here?" Her tone indicated more.

"Seeking his creator, or God of course."

"I thought that's what he is."

"To some he is God. He even thought he was at one period in his development, but now he knows there was one before him even larger that spawn him. He is merely seeking him out beyond the barrier of the Great Darkness following the route he believes the 'Being' took."

"What makes you think I am going to allow myself, or my crew to enter your electromagnetic gun?" She began to feel better knowing she had choices too.

"It will happen. Events have already been put into motion. I can merely prepare you for it."

"Well you can stop! I am not falling for this, or any other psych test you religious radicals are dreaming up. The whole thing is a trick. You work me over when I'm tired and vulnerable, but I am on to you," she said aloud. She felt pleased with herself for catching on. Yet, the imagery and explanation seemed so clear and real. Yes, the High Achievers could be proud of this one. She almost took their bait.

She felt alone. Looking around, the spook was gone, and so was the three "D" image of the whirling black hole and the electromagnetic cord. Only the dome with the star studded black sky remained.

Suddenly blaring over the speaker, Henderson's voice came booming through. "Captain Mc Clure! Captain Mc Clure! Bridge! Bridge! Immediately!"

The voice struck every cell in her brain. Startled, she felt herself being sucked into a small chamber with the sides pressing in on her. Struggling, the pressure increased, causing her head to pound until the pain consumed her whole 'Being'.

The urgency in his voice told her she had to move, but her body was not cooperating. The pressure continued to increase holding her down.

She heard the soft voice again. "Relax, allow your body to adjust. You have been out of body. Your essence must realign itself with your body."

She knew it was Charlie. Finally, she gave in and relaxed. The pressure subsided, but her head continued to throb. Concentrating on the chair in front of her, she tried to focus, but the chair continued to vibrate. Her eyes saw only a blur.

What happened? Did someone drug her? The tingling, vibrating sensation slowly settled down. Maybe she could move her legs. Her mind moved them, but her legs remained in the chair. Frustrated, she tried again, but nothing! "They won't move!" She concentrated harder. She…She saw them sliding toward the floor, or whatever that was vibrating down there.

Touching, she felt something solid. She started to put more weight on her legs, when she found herself falling. The light gravity helped. In slow motion she saw herself dropping to the floor. She hit hard and felt the pain go through her body. She laid there a moment to allow the pain to diffuse.

The speaker blared again, "Captain Mc Clure, emergency!

Bridge! Immediately!"

Concentrating on the hatch across the room, she moved that direction. Crawling at first, then slowly she eased herself up on her knees. Weak, every muscle in her body vibrated. It was like they had fallen asleep from a lack of a blood flow. She picked up the sensation of a million tiny needles poking her.

She had never felt this way before. Using the chair beside her, she struggled to her feet. Like a baby learning to walk, she took two quick steps forward then stopped. Concentrating on the hatch, she tried to focus before trying. Everything continued to vibrate, but not as much. Her legs felt stronger, and the prickling sensation was less. She quickly took ten more steps before flinging herself towards the opening.

Her hands clasped the middle of the vibrating head rail and found something solid. She hung on holding herself up. She felt her wobbly legs becoming stronger. Breathing in deep, her head began to clear, but the pain continued!

It felt like someone had stuffed her brain into a small steel box that now screamed to get out. The pressure slowly decreased, but the ache remained leaving the back of her head throbbing.

She started to fade. Concentrating on the door molding, she brought herself back into focus. Her eyes cleared, the vibrating slowed and finally stopped. Everything appeared normal. Still a bit wobbly she moved through the hatch and down the hall. She held down the need to empty her stomach as she stumbled into the lift. She pressed the up button.

On the Bridge Mr. Henderson whirled around when the lift hatch opened. In it was Ana barely standing with her hair distraught, eyes baggy and dark, clothes distorted, and generally looking like death warmed over. "What happened to you?"

Ana, realizing she was making a bad appearance, yelled, "What do you expect after a forty-eight hour of back to back watches? Then when I am about to close my eyes, a person I know, jerks me out of a sound sleep with his blow horn. This had better be important, Mister!"

"We're at Star Base Twelve, but they won't let us dock."

"Star Base Twelve?" She asked surprised. "We're not supposed to be here until tomorrow."

"It is tomorrow. You've been asleep eighteen hours."

"Eighteen?" She asked startled. "I just laid down a moment ago…Eighteen hours, you sure?"

He pointed to the view screen. "There's Alpha Twelve!"

Shaking her head, she could not believe the eighteen hours. Then straightening herself up, she walked onto the Bridge and took command. "Why won't they let us dock?"

"Something about another Starship. I couldn't quite make it out."

"So what? They're big enough to handle both of us. Tell them we're coming in. They can have the other ship wait."

Mr. Henderson returned to the communication board and shook his head. "Nothing but static."

"Better take us back out a bit, and then try long range."

He nodded and reversed the engines until the space station was a small object on the screen. "How is this, ma'am?"

"Good! Put them on screen."

The screen above the console lit up. A small man wearing a space uniform was barely visible through the static. "Stay back!" He shouted. "Hold your position! Hold your position!"

"What's going on Monzor?"

"The EM-1…" The voice faded along with the image.

"Take us further out Mr. Henderson. They seem to be having communication problems close in."

"Further from what, ma'am? They're gone!"

"What do you mean?"

"The space station has disappeared! They're gone!"

"Say again!"

"The space station has disappeared!" Mr. Henderson said with more emotion. "They're gone!"

"We just had them on screen!"

"I know, ma'am, but now they're gone." He pointed to the empty screen.

"Exploded or what? I didn't feel a shock wave!"

Mr. Henderson began checking the computer sensors. "No explosion, no residue, nothing. Scanning the area, I'm picking up something in orbit 15."

"Probably the other ship. Hail them! See if they saw anything."

Suddenly the screen filled with a tall man dressed in religious robes with his hands folded, "Reverend High Achiever Kole from the Starship EM-1 at your service."

"What is going on? Where is the Captain?"

"The crew transferred to Star Base Twelve," Kole replied in an even voice. "Only the religious contingency remained on board. We have already sent a message back to Star Base Eleven."

"We're coming aboard, Kole! You know only space personnel are allowed to operate starships."

"Yes, we have been expecting your arrival."

Ana, startled, but controlled her composure. "Then lock on us, we're on our way!"

The screen went blank. Ana turned to Henderson, "Well?"

"You did find, ma'am, but I think we should still put a call through to Star Base Eleven. I didn't pick up any transmission."

Ana nodded, and then pushed the General Quarters button. "Let's not take any chances."

Mr. Henderson turned the direction finder toward Star Base Eleven, then looked at Ana with a puzzled look. "Nothing but static, ma'am. Going to audio." Over the speakers the sound of static became louder.

"Shields, Mr. Henderson!" She shouted. "Shields! Send the space capsule now!"

Mr. Henderson started to push a few more buttons when the ship suddenly lost power. The lights in the Bridge blinked twice then went out. The entire ship was left in darkness.

"Battle lanterns! Battle lanterns!" Ana shouted. She looked around quickly, and then at Mr. Henderson when the battle lanterns came on. "Engines, Mr. Henderson?"

"Gone! We're floating without power!"

"Life support?"

"Seems to be holding, but they're on emergency status."

"It has to be coming from that EM-1 ship!"

"We don't know that, ma'am."

"My gut does! Have Parker and Judy meet us in the shuttle bay along with ten security personnel. We're going to board a ship, even if we have to use manual all the way!"

"Lasers?"

"Full complement," she replied going to the locker.

Mr. Henderson smiled, and put the instructions through the emergency communication system. Turning, he followed the Captain down the tube ladder carrying the weapon belts. Reaching the shuttle bay took ten minutes because each door without the ship's power had to be manually opened.

Ana, ahead of Mr. Henderson, opened the last door, she found security already in their unzipped spacesuits waited for their weapons as they helped Judy and Parker with theirs.

Mr. Henderson passed out the weapons as the crew zipped up.

Ana sent four of the security personnel to manually open the outer bay doors and to make the two shuttles ready for lift off.

Parker, halfway in his suit, "I am not cut out for this. Why are you taking me on your little raid?"

Ana turned to Parker, "Need you where the casualties are going to be."

"How about if they shoot back? I could become one of them."

"I was talking about their casualties, Doctor. I don't think a few religious freaks are capable of taking on a military contingency."

"I wouldn't underestimate them, ma'am, I hear they destroyed the space station."

"We don't know that for sure. We're just not taking any chances." Ana, putting on her suit, turned to Ralph Bertrum, one of her security officers with a pilot insignia on his sleeve. He stood a foot taller than her causing her to look up. "After you load the weapons bar lift off immediately. Take up a defensive position. We need some eyes out there now. Move it!"

"Aye, aye, ma'am!" He said turning. He ran for the airlock.

"You'll be on manual!" She shouted after him.

In a few minutes the weapon bar was loaded. The Beta shuttle lifted off. It eased out into the darkness.

Ana, dressed, "Okay, it's our turn! Mr. Henderson, the weapons bar if you please. The rest of you into the shuttle. I don't like being defenseless to whatever it is out there."

The others made their way across the walkway to the shuttle while Mr. Henderson locked in the weapon's bar. The no gravity made the work easy. "There! That should give us some advantage!"

"Good, Mr. Henderson! Now let's move it! I have a feeling we're running short on time."

"Yes ma'am!" He swung himself into the walkway and

entered the shuttle.

Manually firing up the engines, Ana moved them out of the bay doors. The star-studded sky was normal. Beta shuttle held its position on the starboard side a bit in front of them. Then the largest ship she has ever seen, the size of a space station, took up half the view screen. "Look at that, Mr. Henderson!"

"Yes ma'am, but more to the point, what is it?"

"It looks like a huge electric motor, if I remember right."

"You do, ma'am, an electromagnetic one to be exact."

"But where are the crew's quarters and bridge?"

"Maybe in the middle. The electromagnetic part could be built around it."

"Yes! There!" Ana yelled, "Turning toward us! It looks like a Starship in the middle! They're bringing the engines around." She finally realized what was happening. Shouting into the communicator. "Beta, move out to the starboard now! We'll take the port side. Whatever the thing is, it's attacking! Let's not make it easy!"

Over the speaker, "Yes, ma'am!"

She pushed the thrusters to full power shoving the stick to the left. It took them toward the front of the turning craft. Using the screen, she watched the huge spaceship slow. It stopped when the aft section lined up with the spacecraft they had just left. "What are they doing?"

Mr. Henderson moved into the battle chair, unlocked the firing block, "Probably getting ready to fire!"

Ana, into her communicator, "Beta, make a run from your side. Come in after us, we're going for the front of this thing."

Beta shuttle started to answer back when the static took out the screen. Twenty seconds later, the screen cleared, but only the huge ship was visible.

Ana turned the outside camera, surveying the empty space. "I don't see Beta, or our Starship. Check the scanners!"

"Nothing ma'am! Only us and the EM-1."

Ana, into the communicator, shouted, "Beta! Beta! Come in!" Looking back at Mr. Henderson, she realized he was right. Her anger swelled quickly. "Let's fry it!"

Parker, pushing his way forward, yelled, "No you don't! That's our way home! This shuttle can't last more than a week with this many people in it."

"You're right, Doctor! We'll board her first, then fry their royal high hindies!"

"Something odd here, ma'am. The EM-1 is making no attempt to stop us," Mr. Henderson said.

"They haven't opened their bay doors yet to welcome us."

"What would you like, ma'am?"

"A P-torpedo will be sufficient Mr. Henderson."

The doctor pointed, shouting, "You don't need to, ma'am. The door is opening."

The bay door, slowly at first, then increasing its speed, disappeared into the ship's frame.

"So, they are, Doctor, but it still doesn't make them friendly."

Mr. Henderson moved the shuttle through the open bay door. "I don't like this, ma'am! Why didn't they try to blast us out of the sky like they did the others?"

Parker putting in, "Maybe they're giving up. They took their best shot. We just out flanked them."

"No Doctor, no attempt was made. I think Mr. Henderson is right. They are expecting us. They didn't want the others interfering. Their new weapon is very thorough."

The Doctor, not convinced, "I can't believe they killed hundreds on the space station and our ship just to prevent interference."

"We'll know in a minute," Mr. Henderson said setting the shuttle on the empty Beta shuttle pad. "Someone has taken a shuttle out of here. It could have been our missing Captain."

Ana took out her blaster. "We're taking this ship! Shoot anyone who tries to stop us. I'll take Judy and two security, and head for the Bridge. Mr. Henderson, you take Parker, and George. We need control of their engine compartment."

Parker made a painful look, "I think someone should guard the shuttle. Seeing how I am not really fighting material, I think it should be me."

Mr. Henderson gave her a knowing look. "He'll only slow us down."

"Okay Parker, lock her up tight after we leave, but stay in touch through the wrist com."

"Yes ma'am!"

Mr. Henderson lifted his shoe weights. "They're attaching the walkway. You think we still need the weights?"

"No, disconnect," she said, "We can move faster without them. If they choose to play games, they'll have the same difficulties we do."

She heard the sound of rapid clinging noises when the weights hit the deck. "If a door isn't open to you, cut through it with your laser."

"Even the airlock?" George, a young officer, asked.

"Especially the airlock, we have our suits! They may not."

"That's…That's murder!" Parker pleaded.

"And wiping out a space station, and our ship isn't?" Ana asked using a sarcastic voice.

Parker did not have time for a rebuttal. Ana jumped out the door and began moving through the walkway with her team behind her. Some of them had their lasers drawn.

Half way through the walkway they heard a loud buzzing noise. Suddenly their weapons were ripped from their hands attaching themselves to the sides of the walkway.

Mr. Henderson tried to pull his off but found his entire weapon's belt had become attached. In fact, everything made of metal was sticking tight to the walls. The buzzing sound increased, the flexible metal parts of their spacesuits forced them all to the deck.

Ana instinctively unzipped her suit. She was out of it when her suit hit the deck. The others, not as quick, found themselves struggling to do the same on the deck. Looking up, she saw her antagonist, the Reverend High Achiever Kole, smile from behind the protective Plexiglas inside the hatch. Her anger flared. She ran toward him. "She didn't need weapons to wipe that smirk off his face!" But something was wrong! She was going in slow motion. More, she was not touching the deck!

She flung herself out. She managed to clasp the handrail. Looking back, she saw Mr. Henderson out of his suit. His hand was on the stuck laser against the bulkhead of the walkway. He was trying to blast a hole through the lock in front of her, but he was not aiming it properly.

Instead, he was blasting away the walkway. Giving up, he pushed off back toward his suit as the high pressurized walkway became equalized with the vacuum in the shuttle bay.

Ana, further away, was not doing as well. Pulling hard, she could see her suit a good five meters away. The others, already back to their suits, were zipping in. Judy, still in her suit, attempted to break free from the deck. She tried to reach out to Ana, but only her eyes, tearing fast, could move.

Mr. Henderson was not doing better. After zipping himself in, he turned to face her, but he became helpless too. If he left his suit, he died. If he did not, she surely would. He was pointing at something behind her.

She started to turn, when something took her arms. Too weak to resist she managed to see two people in spacesuits before blacking out.

7 The Conversion

Hours later she found herself lying on a strange bed. Soft, not the hard regulation types that folded up in the wall. Covering her was a down quilt, soft, light, and smelling new. Overhead she saw a pink canopy. This was not regulation either.

She raised herself on her elbow, but found her head sunk immediately into a large soft pillow. Managing to sit up, she looked around. Where was she? The room was large with soft pink colors flowing through the feminine textured walls and curtains around her bed. Slowly she became frightened. Was she dead?

She started to swing up out of the bed, when she found herself restricted in a pink flowered nightgown. Somebody had undressed and put her in here, or was she dreaming this?

Pulling the pink comforter back, she swung her legs over

the edge of the bed allowing her bare feet to touch the cold tile. At first, she recoiled. Then she allowed the cold to work its way up her legs. She began to like the reality of the feeling.

Soft music floated on the air. Light, it gave her a little girl feeling. Twirling once, she allowed the music to carry her as she moved across the floor. The music began to increase in volume and tempo. To stay with it she had to move faster using shorter steps until she could no longer float about the room. Instead, she was standing in one place moving every part of her body to keep up with the tempo.

Her deeper aggressions began to surface until it consumed her 'Being'. Jerking in deep extended motions, she followed the music's deep rhythmic beat. It increased in volume and tempo until all she could do was scream her frustrations at her failure to stay with it. Falling to the floor exhausted, she laid face down, and forced her mind to ignore the pounding beat.

Suddenly the loud music stopped. It became soft attempting to work itself back into her mind. She almost allowed it to sooth the pent-up frustrations inside. She wanted it! Actually, she needed it! Something told her this.

The room began to darken. The soft features changed to shadows that took on an ominous feeling. The music changed to deeper tones bringing her up to a sitting position.

Slowly the wall in front of her merged into a whirling black hole. It became larger moving towards her. Quickly she was on her feet. Backing away, she looked around. The bed was gone!

The other walls, growing spikes, began to move toward her. She was being forced into the whirling tunnel.

She did not want to go. She knew what was inside the tunnel. Fear, building fast, wanted to consume her. She held it down. "No! I won't do it!"

Was she shouting? Was there someone else here? She felt better though the tunnel moved closer. "I said I won't do it!" She screamed.

Someone was hearing her. She knew it deep and profound. "Go ahead, let your walls of death do their best. I'm not going!"

The walls became fiery red pressing closer. Yes, they want to burn her again. Again? Yes again! She remembered the closing walls of the black pod. She felt better knowing her fear was generating these images.

The whirling hole faded along with the moving walls leaving her in complete darkness. The tile floor dissolved. She was sinking through the floor. She…She was floating free in the dark. The surge of fear almost caused her to panic, but she controlled it. Was she tumbling? It was hard to tell without walls to orient her.

"Cold!"

Yes, she was cold! Wrapping her arms around herself, she found her nightgown missing. She…She was naked! Now she was hoping the darkness held. Someone was watching her. She could feel it! He was somewhere out there in the darkness.

Keeping her hands ready, she poised herself to take on this new aggressor.

The cold increased, the darkness became thicker, moving in closer. "Are you trying to suffocate me?" She…She could not breathe. Moving her arms, she tried to shove the darkness back to allow the air to enter her lungs. The panic feeling built! "I can't breathe!" She tried to yell, but her voice was barely audible.

Then remembering her mind was doing this, she forced herself to relax. She allowed the huge black chunks to bump, and flow around her body. Yes, she has been through this before. Then shouting, "Is this the best you can do?"

The blackness began to whirl. It moved faster around her. Maybe it wasn't smart to challenge them. Picking up speed, she found herself hurling through the whirling black tunnel. Yes, it was her old dream coming back to haunt her, but she survived it inside the black pod, or did she?

A feeling inside was telling her the black pod was only a prelude to the actual experience in front of her. The speed increased. The stars became blurs. "Stars?" She asked. "What stars? Where did the stars come from?"

Everything was becoming a blur except the whirling mass in front of her. She was descending into a huge black hole. The tidal forces were already working. They wanted to pull her apart. She could feel her feet becoming disconnected.

Quickly tucking herself, she began to roll. She did not like it, but her compact size lowered the tidal forces. Looking up, she could see the end of the deep funnel. It was a large hole of glaring light. The pressure continued to build. It compacted her tighter.

Now she wanted out of the tuck position, but she could not move. It became even tighter. She was blending into herself! She…She was…The pressure on her head…Was pushing her down. It was forcing her out of her body.

Vibrating! Her body was vibrating faster! She was leaving her body! She could feel herself half way out of it! She tried to hold on, but the pressure was greater. Closing her eyes tighter, she reached back for more of her. It was not helping! She was slipping. She felt herself stretching.

Suddenly she snapped free. The pressure was gone. She…She was floating free. She did not dare open her eyes. She did not want to admit she was dead. She allowed herself to float in the warm air.

Nothing could hurt her now. Strange how this entered her mind, she thought. Dimly she wondered where it came from. She did not really care. She was feeling peaceful and free. "I tried to stay alive, didn't I? I did all I could. They wouldn't let me."

She worked the guilt down into her subconscious. She felt better. Yes, it was all so peaceful. She wondered why she tried to resist.

She heard voices! Curious, she concentrated, picking up Parker's voice. "Was he dead too?"

"Open your eyes," A voice closer to her said.

Whirling around to the voice, she asked, "Who…Who said that? Do I know you?"

"You called me Charlie," the voice said calmly, "Open your eyes please."

"No! I don't want to!" She said fearing she might not be able to. She was dead. Dead people don't see.

"Nothing will hurt you," the voice said calmly. "Open your eyes please."

"I don't have any eyes. They're back in my body. I'm dead! Didn't they tell you?"

"No, you are not dead, only out of your body. Now, open your eyes, and see with your inner eyes."

"How do I know you're, Charlie?"

"You know. Now open your eyes and look at me."

Forcing herself, she allowed a small amount of light into her safe blackness.

"More! I am right here beside you."

Letting more light in, she saw an orange ball of mist floating in front of her. "Okay, so you're Charlie, but I still don't talk to spooks!"

"What do you think you look like?"

"I have a body…I can…"

"No, you are a floating mist like me, communicating telepathically if we must use your terms, but actually we pick up each other's thoughts."

"How do I see you if I haven't any eyes?"

"Through your inner eyes. In your body you call it a sense. Relying on your physical vision, you have not developed it of course. Even now you only see one direction like your physical eyes. Actually, you can see all directions at once, with depth, and additional dimensions, but that will come."

Opening more, she began to see the sides of a Spaceship. Looking around, she noticed she was floating ten feet off the floor. Instinctively she went down fearing she would fall.

Charlie remained where he was at. "Come back please," he said in a soft voice. "Surely you are used to free fall."

"Yes, when I have my body."

"Hympt! That is when it is the most difficult."

"How do I get there without a thruster pack?"

"Simply think here, or better, simply come here."

"I am thinking, but nothing is happening."

"In your body, how do you raise your arm?"

"I don't know I just move it."

"Yes, you move it where you want to put it. So now think where you want to be, then let your essences go there."

Ana started to concentrate, but before she could close her inner eyes, she was beside Charlie. "How did I do that?"

"You make things way too complicated, my dear."

Ana started to say something, when she heard other voices coming from the far side of the compartment. Four men dressed in long white togas were staring down at something pulled out of the wall. A fifth man dressed in regulation service uniform was…Parker. He was arguing with them. She started to move closer.

Charlie quickly moved out in front of her. "Maybe you should do some exploring first before going over there."

"What are they looking at? What's Parker doing here?"

"You!"

"Me?" Going around Charlie, she quickly floated to the pulled-out drawer, and stopped four feet above the body. She could only stare at herself. She felt so alien from the body below her. "I'm…I'm in a psych tank! My clothes! Where are my clothes?" She watched Parker turn to the others.

"She's gone Reverend High Achiever," Parker said in a low

voice. "I can't bring her back. The tank only works while she is in her dream state."

The tall Reverend High Achiever Kole did not like the loss. "I thought you controlled the dream state. How could she leave?"

"I don't know. It has never happened before. All I can tell you, she's gone. She doesn't respond to anything."

"Is she dead?" Kole asked.

"No, but damn close to it, more like a comatose state."

"Then I suggest we wait until she chooses to come back. We have the executive officer I believe."

Parker nodded toward the Neoann shuttle crew on the deck beside the drawer. "He's over there, but she's the stronger of the two."

"Your report stated she has fear of the darkness, but I did not see any sign of it in the tank."

"I'm telling you," he said loudly, "She is!"

"Maybe you need some tank time, Doctor," Kole said. He turned and walked over to Mr. Henderson. Looking down, "How does he hold up under pressure?"

The Doctor lowered his head. "Good, but she is far the superior."

"Then I say we wait for her," Kole replied and turned back

to Ana. "Take her to my quarters. Let her emergence be in a nice setting. We are not inhuman here."

Reverend Kenzie, short, overweight, looked up meekly at the High Achiever Kole. "What about their conversions?"

"Ah yes, you will continue the conversion process on the others, Doctor," Kole replied turning back to Parker. "We will all be one in the spirit when we enter the Gate to Heaven."

"Captain Mc Clure?" Parker asked.

"Oh, we have a special conversion process for her. Since she is not susceptible to the conversion container, then her conversion will be a natural and permanent one. It will be done by God, our Lord and Savior, in the Hall of Life."

The other three High Achievers carefully lifted Ana's body from the drawer and followed the Reverend High Achiever Kole out the door.

The doctor watched them leave while he slowly closed the empty drawer.

Ana, coming out of her trans-state, started after them, but she was cut off by the sliding hatch. Turning, she faced Charlie coming up behind her. "I want my body back!" She demanded.

"Yes, my dear, anytime you are ready."

"Then how do I get this hatch open?"

"You do not without a body. Do you remember the reddish

orange essence from the black pod? How she moved through the metal plates of your ship? You can do the same in this state if you like."

She turned and threw herself hard into the bulkhead. Suddenly her whole 'Being' was filled with pain. She floated slowly back to Charlie. She could feel her whole essence swelling. "I hurt! God, I hurt! I didn't think that was possible once I was dead."

"Whoever told you that?" Charlie asked. "You can be hurt indeed! More so, because your body does not buffer you. Now, if you will just ease yourself through, you will find it quite painless."

Feeling better, more determined, she tried again, and found herself dissolving into the bulkhead. She could feel the metal. Every fiber of it was meshing with her essence. She felt a tingling sensation increasing in intensity. It was going to consume her! She wanted out. Quickly turning, she pulled herself back to Charlie. "I can't do it."

"Try again but think only part of yourself through. You must thin out. You are trying to force the metal wall through you instead of you through the wall"

"Okay Charlie, you get one more try. It better work!" She moved towards the wall.

"Now think the other side," he said. "Visualize the passageway and let yourself go."

She allowed her mind to see the passageway. Hazy at first, but it began to clear. Now she could see both sides of the hatch. It depended on what side she focused on. "Now what?" She felt something push her. It was Charlie. She found herself fully focused in the passageway with Charlie beside her. She could feel Charlie smiling.

"See, not so bad."

She started to reply when her mind remembered why she wanted through. Leaving him behind, she quickly moved down the hall, slipping through the other bulkhead.

Charlie, impressed by her ability, stayed behind. "Yes, she does learn fast. I think our Doctor is going to be in for a rough time."

Coming through the wall, Ana slowed, then hovered near the top of the ceiling. On the bed below, her body laid motionlessly. It was the same bed she saw in her dream even down to the pink lace.

Two of the High Achievers slipped the pink quilt comforter over her body gently, then left the room.

Reverend Kenzie stood beside Reverend High Achiever Kole waiting for the black body to come back to life. Then breaking the silence, he said, "Maybe we should have left her with Doctor Parker."

"No, either she will recover here, or she will die here," Kole replied. "Like the good doctor said, it is out of his hands. Now it is out of ours. We no longer control." Slowly he turned leaving the room with Reverend Kenzie following.

Ana waited until the sliding door closed, then she moved towards her body. She had no idea how to get back inside.

"You let yourself fall back in," Charlie said coming through the door. "Though maybe for the first time you should lie down beside it and roll in."

She wanted inside her body! The urge, becoming stronger, overcame her fear. She followed directions. Lying down, she rolled in. Suddenly her body began to vibrate or was it her vibrating. It frightened her, she rolled back out. "It doesn't want me!" She yelled. "My body doesn't want me!"

"Yes, it does, but you must relax," Charlie said reassuring her. "Give your body's wave time to adjust, to become one with you again. Then the shaking will stop."

Tensing, she forced herself back to the body. Slowly she rolled back into the vibrations. Holding, she forced herself to stay, and heard Charlie's voice coming through the mist.

"Relax! Relax, let it happen."

It was working. The vibrations began to slow. She felt herself lining up with her wave. When it came into sync, she felt herself fall in. She wanted to sit up, but she felt apprehensive thinking she might come back out. She did not dare open her eyes. They were glued shut.

She heard Charlie's voice. "You can sit up, but I would suggest very slowly. A quick movement may take you back out some causing your brain to lose its guide. In other words, you may faint."

She continued to lie there. It was all right. She was not going anywhere fast. Her body felt like a thousand pounds. She could barely move. Edging herself toward the edge of the bed, she tried to sit up only to find her head spinning. Dropping her head, she waited for it to clear. She began to realize how heavy her body was.

"Try it slower," Charlie said.

Determined, she sat up, forcing herself to her feet by using the bed for support. She waited for the spinning to stop. She remembered doing this before after her last lesson in the dome room. She felt the pressure mounting in her head. "Am I going to have a headache like the last time?" She asked.

"If you push it. Your body has to adjust slowly."

Standing, she held the rail, and tried to open her eyes. Pushing, she forced one eye then the other. Focusing, she realized she was naked.

Suddenly she felt Charlie watching her. She needed her clothes! She needed them now!

Looking around the room, she noticed a closet of sorts through the mist whirling around her head. Forcing herself, using the bed and walls, she staggered to a panel with the word

'Locker' above it. Opening, all she could find were togas. The only feminine one left her with a bare shoulder.

It took her five minutes to figure it out, but she managed to put it on. The effort also allowed her body to become more coordinated. She started with fat thumbs and focus problems, now she began to see objects clearer.

Then remembering Charlie, she whirled. He was gone! Maybe by being in her body she couldn't see him. No, her senses told her the room was empty. He probably picked up on her embarrassment and left the room.

It didn't matter. She was back in her body. Strange, she felt all right except for a slight burning sensation in her lower stomach area. Her mind flashed through the possibilities. "No, they wouldn't do anything like that," she thought. Not wanting to think about it, she closed her mind, and headed for the door. It was time to pay our good doctor a visit.

Going back through the hall, she tried to remember which hatch she went through. "Strange how different things look from this perspective," she thought. The sign above her read,

"Medical."

She pushed the button, the door slid open. Stepping through, she stopped abruptly, in front of her stood her crew except for two of her security officers.

Doctor Parker, noticing her, turned slowly. "Aw, how beautiful we look."

"Can it, Parker! I know what you've been up to!"

"My dear, we have been waiting for you," Parker replied.

She looked from one to the other. They all had a smile on their face, even Judy. "I can see you have. Now, how about turning these village idiots back too normal?"

"They are normal. It is you who needs the transformation."

Quickly her mind began to register. Parker was one of them! He always has been! She remembered her earlier thoughts. Yes, her ship had a mole. Why did she believe hers would be the exception? Of course, it would take one familiar with psych tanks. All these thoughts took only seconds. She had to bluff! "I am transformed!" She lifted her arm showing the white hanging garment. "I was just checking out the rest of you."

"Yes ma'am, maybe you are." He started to say more, when the communicator lit up on his wrist. He lifted it to his ear, then he looked at Ana. Nodding his head, he pressed it again, turning it off. "It appears his High Achiever wants' you to meet the creator from whom all life comes for your true conversion."

Ana began to back away. "No, I am already converted, the same as the rest of you!"

Smiling, they approached her. Mr. Henderson stepped in front of the door to stop any quick escape.

Parker shook his head, "No, you didn't take in the psych

tank. Yours' will have to be direct. Sorry ma'am, but it is the only way."

"Parker, you're a traitor. These are your own crewmates! I am your captain. You are a doctor! How can you ethically turn us all into zombies?"

"Not zombies' ma'am, but part of the Creator. He will guide us into eternity. He says we must all be of one spirit when we enter the 'Gate to Heaven'."

"What are you talking about, Parker? All I see is a bunch of religious freaks destroying a space station, and our own Starship killing I don't know how many people. Now you talk like this doesn't matter. You're in the Star Command, Parker! Don't let these religious freaks get away with this."

"There are always sacrifices one must make, ma'am, to obtain one's goals. You will understand soon."

"No! Your goon patrol here may take me anywhere they wish, but I'm not joining anything alive or dead."

Judy spoke up, "No, Captain, you have it all wrong. It's a pleasant feeling. It feels like a ton of bricks being lifted from your soul. Can't you feel the energy in this ship? Every pore reeks of it."

Suddenly behind Mr. Henderson the door slid open. The Reverend High Achiever Kole with two of his disciples entered. He looked at Ana, and then the rest of the crew. "I think we have a ship to run. It is time we left this orbit to seek out the

'Gate to Heaven'."

Ana glared at him, "You mean hell, don't you! My crew isn't taking this ship anywhere except maybe back to the Star Fleet Command."

The Reverend High Achiever studied her a second. "I think we still need some retraining, Doctor."

"No, I'm not getting into one of your tanks!" Ana said backing away.

"No, we know the conversion chamber did not take on you, but this will not stop us from seeking the 'Gate to Heaven'."

"You will find I can be very uncooperative." Ana said defiantly.

"Yes, so it seems," Reverend Kole said. Then lowering his voice, he said, "Take her, and follow me!"

His two disciples, big strong muscular types, quickly took Ana by the arms. They lifted her off the deck and proceeded out the door behind the Reverend High Achiever.

Parker watched the door close, turned to the others, "I think it prudent we take our stations immediately."

The others nodded filing out leaving the doctor to himself. Biting his lip, he turned, and walked back to the psych tanks. There were some adjustments he needed to make. He did not like the idea of almost losing his Captain.

Two security personnel from Ana's ship stood next to an airlock on the flight deck several decks up. They were wearing space gear. This included spacesuits, emergency pack, extra air tanks, but no thrusters.

Taking up positions around the two, were ten disciples dressed in white togas. They waited for the Reverend High Achiever. The door to the compartment slid open. Immediately they came to attention.

The Reverend High Achiever entered. He looked at the two Neoann security men in spacesuits, then he turned to watch Ana being lifted through the hatch by his two large disciples. They deposited her on the deck in front of the two security men and stood back.

Ana looked up at the Reverend High Achiever, "You plan to throw me out the airlock?"

"Why no, my dear, we are not barbarians." He turned to the disciples and nodded.

Four disciples quickly pushed pass Ana and placed the two security men in the airlock. Stepping back, they closed the door, and pressed the first button.

Ana, realizing what was about to happen, rolled to her feet. She leaped at the one about to push the second button. Both tumbled to the floor. On her feet quickly, she managed to take out four more before the remaining eight subdued her.

Holding each appendage, they brought her face to face

with the Reverend High Achiever. "You didn't disappoint me, my dear. I expected a gallant effort to save your men." Then glancing at the disciple closes to the airlock's second button, he said, "If you would be so kind."

"What kind of monster are you?" Ana yelled struggling to free herself, but to no avail. The confines of her toga made it difficult for her to maneuver. "Those men can't survive out there!"

"They can survive for twelve hours. The time we need to transverse the gate, and for you to come back here to rescue them," Kole replied calmly.

"What are you talking about? All I see is you murdering two good men, and it appears taking great pleasure in their suffering."

"No, I am giving them a chance to survive if you cooperate." He nodded, and the disciple pushed the second button sending the two men hurling out into space.

Ana could see their eyes pleading for her to do something before they disappeared into the darkness. Glaring at the Reverend High Achiever, she yelled, "You have just killed them, a slow torturous death. It would have been kinder to do it quickly."

"You are being harsh, my dear," Kole replied in a calm voice. "No, you can rescue them when you return saying you are as good as we have been led to believe."

"Have you ever tried to find something out here?"

"They have a transponder that should help, and we plan to travel faster than the speed of light shortly. You may even gain some additional time if the old theories prove correct. Maybe arrive back here before our departure."

"You hit it right when you said old theories. They have never been proven."

"Well, you will have the opportunity now that you have the proper incentive." He nodded, and the disciples released her.

Straightening her toga, she turned back to Kole, "This had better work, or I'll be coming after you personally."

"Threats again, will you ever learn, my dear?"

"Don't call me dear! I'm not one of your religious concubines! Go dear someone else!"

"Do not be so hasty, my dear," Kole said ignoring her comment. "Mmmm. I like your spirit! Yes, I think we have a chance now. If you will follow me, I will show you to the Bridge. Admittedly I know very little about it."

"Then you won't be throwing me out?"

"We have Mr. Henderson, but since he has been in the conversion chamber, we are not sure how much knowledge we may have erased. We may have taken out something vital to run the ship. It would be nothing critical except in an emergency where experience comes into play."

"And if I don't cooperate?"

"You lose the men outside, and as many of your crew until you decide it is worthwhile."

"Might not be a bad idea if you start with Parker!"

"We are humorous." He turned and led the disciples and Ana out of the room.

8 The Gate to Heaven

The religious contingency and Ana stepped into the lift, and ascended to the Bridge. Mr. Henderson and crew were already checking the equipment when they entered.

Mr. Henderson turned, smiled, "Nice to see the Captain is joining us."

Ana, in an irritated voice, said, "Wipe that stupid grin off your face, Mister. I'll not be having my crew acting like religious freaks even if they are!"

Obviously hurt, he dropped the smile from his face, "Whatever pleases the Captain."

"That goes for the rest of you too! You can still act like Starship Officers!"

Behind her the Reverend High Achiever said, "They are

only children in the Lord, my dear. We must have patience."

Ana whirled on him, "Are you going to be on this deck too?"

"From time to time," Kole replied.

"I don't like any of you religious freaks up here! You don't know what you're doing. You might accidentally do something to jeopardize the mission. At the very least you will interfere with us doing our job."

"I see your point. We will allow you your privacy, but we will monitor your progress from below. Try something foolish, and you will lose your two crew members plus whoever else it will take for your complete cooperation."

"Are you going to put us on video?"

"Will that be necessary?"

"No."

"Then we will not!" With that the Reverend High Achiever Kole motioned to his contingency of followers and led them back into the lift.

When the door closed, Ana breathed in deep. She allowed the air to escape slowly. "Nice to have that one off your back," then turning to Mr. Henderson, "Have you figured out how they operate this thing yet?"

"I believe so, ma'am. It's a standard Starship locked into this huge circular electromagnetic ring. I am not sure what is holding it in the ring. My best guess is a magnetic lock of some sort."

"Is there a way to unlock the EM ring?"

"Haven't found it yet, Judy is still looking."

Judy turned, smiled, "Not yet, Brother Henderson, but I will keep looking," she said in a relaxed friendly matter.

Ana quickly became irritated, shouting, "He's not your brother, Young Lady! It's sir to you!"

"Yes ma'am, anything to please the Captain," she replied in a hurt voice.

"And take that silly grin off your face! You better take this more serious, or we may not be getting off this ship!"

"We're going to heaven!" Judy replied. "Who would want to get off?"

"Gees, this is going to be harder than I thought! Just keep looking!"

"What exactly am I looking for ma'am?" Judy asked.

"Something that looks out of place, a switch, a button, you will know when you see it."

Judy's face took on a puzzle look. She did not understand why her Captain wanted to disengage the ship from the EM core portion, especially since it was the part that would take them to heaven.

Mr. Henderson came to the rescue, "Could be they didn't plan to disengage the ship."

"There is a way to break loose from this thing, and I'll do it even if I have to go outside and pry it loose. My gut tells me we may not be coming back if we don't figure it out before we reach this gate, or whatever the Reverend High Achiever calls it."

"It's actually a black hole, at least as far as I can figure out from the charts. See, this is the course set in the computer," he said handing her the ship's docket. Actually, it was a small view screen tied into the main computer.

She pressed a few buttons. a long tubular string was coming out of a whirling black hole, "Better put this up on the big screen, Mr. Henderson."

George, a young man with a quiet sensitive side, was the only remaining security officer. He stopped shifting through the ship's log, and the big screen above the console lit up. "That's it! That's what they have been talking about!"

Ana turned his direction, "What do you have there, George?"

"The worm hole! See, it leads straight into that black hole. It says here they detected it eight years ago. It has been getting closer ever since. They built this ship to enter it, or rather the EM portion of it. To save time," he said looking up, "They made it fit a Starship."

"What's getting closer?"

"The wormhole! That's why we have been orbiting here."

"It's coming here?"

"Supposed to be here now."

Ana snapped at Henderson, "Outside camera!"

Henderson switched to the bow camera. The star-studded darkness filled the screen.

Ana, staring intently, "I don't see anything, Mr. Henderson."

"I doubt if we could see it at first. It will probably be a disturbance of some sort. Let's see here." He began adjusting a few dials. "Here's a picture of the electromagnetic waves out there."

The screen changed to light gray with a darker whirling mass trailing off taking shape.

George, pointing, yelled, "That's it! An electromagnetic tunnel! I think we're supposed to enter that."

Ana, staring, could not say a word. The earlier images of the whirling black hole began to form in her mind. Dimly she heard George continuing.

"They think it leads to a black hole on the other side of the universe, or something that is sucking in a lot of matter. They've seen whole galaxies moving that direction. It says here the Religious Order believes it to be the Gate to Heaven, but the scientific boys' just want to see what it is. Then when the worm hole began to move our direction, they believed it could be used to get there."

Henderson, listening, "How fast will we be going?"

"They don't know. Well beyond the speed of light. It would have to, or we would never reach it," George replied.

Ana shook her head. Then in monotone voice she said, "Yes, well beyond that. We will be shooting through the eye of the black hole at a speed to neutralize the effect of the tidal forces, and the crushing gravity. We will be like an electron in an electromagnetic gun. They believe it will work."

The three turned her direction and stared.

Coming out of her trance, she looked around. She felt awkward. Immediately she took the offensive. "Let's see what we have here, Mr. Henderson. Can you figure out how to start the EM wave?"

"I was hoping George would find it in the manual." Mr. Henderson said moving to a bank of buttons on the left side of the bulkhead. "Now this has been added recently. There's nothing to disconnect us, but maybe to start the wave." He began to analyze the panel underneath.

"It's here!" George said, opening the manual wider. "Yes, the whole bank is it. It says right side for building the field, and left side for taking it down."

Henderson opened the compartment more, removed two covers, and then said quietly, "Yes, it's here. Easy, once you see it."

Ana looked up at the screen, "The worm hole is still moving our direction, Mr. Henderson. Can you operate the EM board?"

"Maybe, if I can find the manual override."

"What do you mean?"

"It's all automatic. It appears the computer operates it."

Ana came back to George. "Why is that wormhole heading our direction? Does the manual say anything?"

"I'm looking! Here's something from the other crew. It's from a Captain Craine. Do you want me to open it?"

"Yes George, anytime you wish," she said trying to keep calm. "Judy, how much time before that wormhole reaches us?"

"Thirty minutes if we don't move."

"Okay George, I think we're in a hurry."

"Maybe you better take this, Captain." He handed her the log disc.

Ana took it and gave it to Henderson. "Let's hear it!"

He slipped the disc into the computer log, pressed the button, and a low muffled voice came over the speakers.

"Captain Randoph Craine, Star Fleet Command, serial

number 305-089-578. Must hurry! I feel it watching me. I am pretending to be entering the log notes, will try to escape with the Beta shuttle to Star Base Twelve. Must stop this! Maybe…Maybe…It's watching me closer. My crew has become part of it. Call themselves disciples of God. I'm locked out of the computer. I no longer control the ship. They put Mr. Gossen in the conversion tank ten minutes ago. It has them all except me.

I see it now, hovering in midair, a white energy field with strips of pink flowing through it. It's moving toward me. It's the first time I've actually seen it. It's closer! God! It knows what I'm thinking! I'm sure of it! Can't…Can't…The log! Yes, the log is finished…Yes…"

The disc went blank. Ana felt nervous. She looked around quickly. "Anymore, Mr. Henderson?"

"No!"

"He may have made it. Beta shuttle was missing when we came in," she said.

"We must continue the count down," Henderson said in a controlled voice.

"No, we pull back until we figure out what's going on here. Judy, impulse power if you please, and then a hard right at flank speed."

Judy started to press the power button, when suddenly the

whole bank lit up. The ship moved forward, and gradually began to pick up speed.

Ana smiled, "Nice, Judy."

Judy, still looking at the board, said, "I…I didn't do it! It…It started by itself."

"Hard right, Judy!" Ana yelled. "Hard right!"

Judy wanted to try, but she could not do it. Her eyes stared at the button, but her hands were unable to move.

Ana ran over, pushed her aside, and began pushing the buttons herself, but the ship continued to move forward towards the whirling worm hole.

Soft music started over the speakers with a slow definite rhythmic pulse. Gradually it increased in volume and intensity.

Ana ignored it and tried desperately to disconnect the power. "Henderson, ax please. Let's smash this computer."

Henderson did not answer.

"The ax, Mr. Henderson," she said reaching for the locker herself. "We're taking our ship back if we have to…" She stopped when she noticed the three of them watching her with blank stares. Slowly she backed away toward the bow of the ship. "Mr. Henderson! Judy! George! What's wrong with you? This thing, whatever it is, controls the ship. You heard Craine!"

Henderson, his voice a slow monotone, "We heard a man

near a mental breakdown refusing to enter the psych tank and run. Now we see a mad woman wanting to smash a perfectly good computer, the life line of the ship. I think you have finally shifted over the edge, ma'am."

"No…No! Look at you three! You have been programmed. You talk funny! You act different!"

"No, we have all been prepared for the journey through God's gateway except you. You said yourself the conversion didn't take. The very thought of moving through a wormhole at speeds beyond the mind of humans has been too much for you," Mr. Henderson said. Hesitating a second, he continued in a soft voice. "Perhaps the problem is the unknown beyond the black hole."

"Henderson, think!" She shouted. "Reach back to the real you! Try! I'm your Captain!" Turning to Judy! "It's me! Tell him!"

Judy, puzzled, looked at her, "Sorry ma'am, but I agree with Mr. Henderson. I…I think he should take charge. I…I'm sorry, but I think it is best for everyone. Maybe you should go try the psych tank again."

George picked up the manual and gave it to Henderson. "There's a sealed hologram disc in here. It says to play it before we enter the gate."

Henderson took the disc and analyzed the seal. "Star Command's insignia," he said and broke the seal. He took out the disc, looked at it once, then placed it in the drive.

The computer hummed a few seconds. Then a hologram of a middle age, heavy shoulder, hard face woman appeared. She was dressed in a flowing blue silk dress. It was the Ma'am High Achiever Monzor, the president of the Federation, floating in the middle of the room. She faced the four of them. Ana knew her immediately. It was the woman who gave her the command of her Starship.

In a deep voice she said, "Congratulation from the Republic, and the High Order of Reverend Achievers. You have been selected, Captain Craine, to lead the chosen few through the 'Gate to Heaven.' This is an important opportunity for mankind. An event we must not fail to take advantage of it. We will monitor your progress as far as we can through the Alpha Twelve Space Station. We all wish you the best of luck and God's speed."

The image dissolved, and the Bridge became quiet. Slowly Ana backed her way towards the elevator. The three continued to watch, but none made a move to stop her.

When the lift door opened, Ana whirled. She came face to face with the Reverend High Achiever Kole and Reverend Kenzie. They advanced forcing her back toward the other three.

The Reverend High Achiever Kole spoke first, "I think it's time for your conversion, my dear. I can see now it was a mistake to delay."

"Yes, that would suit your purpose fine. What did you do with Captain Craine, cast him adrift like my crew?"

"Captain Craine choose his own destruction."

"I bet!"

"We all make choices."

"Yes, well here's mine!" She said darting past the Reverend High Achiever. She met Reverend Kenzie blocking the lift, "Out of my way little man!"

Reverend Kenzie, his voice low, and full of authority, "You cannot escape the wrath of God! Bow down before him. Repent of your sins! Then you may enter the 'Gate to Heaven'".

"I said out of my way, buster!" She lowered her shoulder striking him in the stomach. Pivoting, she was around him and in the lift. She depressed the button, and watched the others trying to reach her. The crumbling body of Reverend Kenzie's blocked their path. The hatch closed, she started down.

Listening to the hum of the lift, she had only seconds to find a spot they could not find. Her mind remembered Judy's comment earlier. "Every pore of the ship reeks with his energy." Whatever this thing is, it can go through walls. Did Craine make it? He figured the flight deck to be the answer.

She took the lift all the way to the bottom. While it was descending, she took off the confining toga. Naked, but she didn't care. At least she could move. When the door slid open, she flung herself out in a defensive position ready to take on any of the new disciples. The others had training. They were probably from Craine's crew, the reason they defeated her so easily earlier.

The speakers blared. "Captain Mc Clure, you cannot escape me. My eyes see all!" It was the Reverend Kenzie's voice.

"He must be the channel," she thought, "For whatever this thing is."

"How about outside the ship?" she asked herself. "Does it see that?" Picking up speed, she moved down the hall. Rounding the corner, she saw the forward locker room. It led to the airlock. She heard a rush of air behind her. It became louder. It was approaching fast. She knew what the sound meant. Someone was purifying the lower deck. They were blowing the air out along with her life-giving oxygen. "Clever, Mr. Henderson," she said to herself.

Reaching the locker door, she found it locked. The automatic switch was off. Going to manual, she jerked the plate loose, and began cranking the door apart.

The rushing air hit her, but the opening was large enough. She took one last large breath, pulled hard, and managed to wedge herself through the door.

Before she could secure the door, the air in the locker room rushed out. This left only the spacesuits with air. She opened the first locker, but she did not bother pulling the suit out. Reaching in, she released the oxygen inside. Quickly she took a couple of deep breaths, closed it off, and looked around. "I must close the door first," she thought.

After cranking it close, she opened more of the suits filling the small compartment with air. Feeling better, she began closing them off. "No sense in wasting the precious commodity," she thought. Finding a uniform that fitted, she quickly placed it over her body. "One must look decent even if it's only a spook who finds her."

She had only seconds before they would figure out she made it inside the locker room. Picking a spacesuit, she quickly donned it. She took a life line and stepped into the airlock.

"Here goes," she said. Taking a deep breath, she depressed the buttons. The outer door opened. It revealed the star filled sky, and the approaching whirling hole. She was hypnotized a few seconds watching it approach. They will have no trouble seeing it now, she thought.

Shaking it off, she needed to work fast. Attaching the life line, she allowed the airlock to close. Suddenly a rush of loneliness filled her mind. She felt herself being cut off from the security inside. Pushing off, she felt the emotion intensifying as she watched the ship drift away. Then suddenly she was jerked back to reality when her life line took hold.

Inside Mr. Henderson looked up at the Reverend High

Achiever, "She has taken a spacesuit, and left the ship through the port airlock."

"Too bad we could not restrain her," The Reverend Kole replied. "She was worth converting. This is truly a great loss. It is my fault. I did not realize how close to the breaking point she was."

"Wormhole coming up!" Mr. Henderson said. He did not want to dwell on it bringing them back to the process at hand.

All except Judy responded. She was no longer functioning. She believed her Captain had just committed suicide. She knew it would be slow and painful. She tearfully looked up at Mr. Henderson. "Can…Can we go back for her? I am sure she will be more cooperative now."

The Reverend Kenzie, broke in. "She had her chance. She chose not to accept God's gift. Now she will be cast out of heaven forever."

Reverend High Achiever Kole placed his arm around her trying to console her. "She has a knack for surviving, my dear. She has her spacesuit. She is still alive somewhere out there. At least you are safe. I am sure she is pleased with that."

Judy looked up at him. She broke out into a new set of tears.

Outside, Ana was pulling herself along the skin of the ship. The huge EM portion, dwarfing the Starship, was small compared to the approaching whirling hole. She glanced at the hole through the side of her head plate. She didn't dare look at it straight on this close. She might become hypnotized by it. She remembered her dream. "No, I must concentrate on business before I can seek the safety inside," she said to herself.

Reaching the area where the EM portion started, she began to analyze the construction. It was a large circular metal ring with the Starship in the very center, but what held the Starship. She did not see any supports coming from the EM unit to the Starship. In fact, a gap of two meters existed between the two with the Starship position exactly in the center.

"It must be magnetic!" She thought. The positive charging units placed evenly inside the ship, held it. It became more so when the EM portion started increasing the negative charge. It would have to be to hold together during the ride through the wormhole.

Her ears began to ring. She quickly turned the audio portion of her suit off. She looked up at the EM Unit. "They are starting it up!"

Turning back toward the bow, she saw the wormhole about to engulf the ship. She needed to get back to her airlock before it did. She knew the acceleration would tear her off the ship whether she had a life line or not.

Kicking off from the side, she swung forward in an arc going out the full length of the line. In seconds that seemed like hours, she finally hit the ship. She worked herself back slipping into the airlock as the EM Unit was winding up to full charge.

The ship curved inward forward of the airlock. It allowed her to look down the throat of the wormhole. A huge mouth of whirling energy, five kilometers in diameter, flashed with lightning, and reached out to them.

Slowly the ship approached until all she could see was the huge mouth about to devour them. The humming noise of the EM unit behind her became louder. Her mind quickly reasoned, "There's no air in space to carry the sound. It must be the whole ship vibrating."

She felt her heart pumping fast along with the other anxiety symptoms one dealt with before they rode a scary roller coaster. She tried to find a more comfortable spot in her spacesuit to accommodate the acceleration she knew was about to take place. Could a Human 'Being' survive? She was about to find out!

9 Heaven

More electrical discharges circled the ship blinding Ana. All she could see was the flashing white. Suddenly the ship jerked forward. It picked up speed continuing to accelerate. She waited for it to stop, but it didn't. Instead, it pinned her tighter against the bulkhead behind her. There was no noise. The vibration had ceased. Only the silence and the acceleration were left.

She felt herself being pushed from her body. She tried to resist, but the force was stronger. She found herself outside her spacesuit. Her body remained, but her mind or thinking part was outside. Frightened, she didn't understand. She tried to get back inside the spacesuit.

"The acceleration prevents it." A voice said.

Startled, she whirled around, trying to locate it. "Where are you?" She demanded.

"Behind you, I exist only as a small portion," the voice said.

Coming around, she saw a small hovering orange mist. "Where have you been, Charlie?"

"I have been hiding in the doctor's body."

"That had to be difficult."

"No, he is rather a nice person."

"Medical fiend, you mean!"

"Do you wish to stay out here and watch, or go inside?" He asked, bringing the conversation back to the problem at hand.

"Watch what? The blur beside us?"

"Those are stars. Soon they will be galaxies. The speed will become enormous."

"At this speed how will we stop?"

"When you pass through the eye of the black hole, you will be taking a portion of his fabric with you. It will act like a brake. Gradually it will slow you down on the other side. You will have a slight delay, and then you and his fabric will return by accelerating back through. Once you are back on this side, you will slow again, and come to rest where you started."

"It's all that easy?"

"No, it's all theory. As I said before it has never been tried, but we believe it will work."

"That sure gives one a lot of confidence." The flashing lights became more of a blur causing her to become more upset. She looked at her unconscious body. It was pressed hard against the bulkhead. She was ready to leave. "I…I think…"

"Yes, we will go inside. Remember to ease yourself through the wall."

Watching Charlie, she started to follow, only to find the bulk of her unable to.

"Thin out, disperse your fabric. Think the whole wall not the small portion you presently have in your mind. It is your tunnel vision stopping you."

She tried again, but this time she relaxed and slipped through. She found Charlie on the other side. The ship seemed cold and quiet. They moved through the passages where only the flickering emergency lights were working. She looked around cautiously. The ship was on emergency life support.

"It is!" Charlie replied reading her mind. "The EM portion disrupts your circuits. I believe you discovered that earlier."

"Yes, but I didn't realize they had to shut down too when they turned the EM on. That would explain why they delayed their attack."

By staying close to Charlie, the transition through the walls was easier. Easing themselves up through the decks, they entered the Bridge. Quiet, everyone was strapped in, but their essence had left his or her body. Only an unconscious heap of human tissue was left behind.

"Where did everyone go?"

"They are here. They have slipped beyond the veil for protection." Charlie picked up the puzzled feeling in Ana. "They are unconscious, but they continue to be close to their bodies. Now I must leave you, and check on the good doctor's body, he seems to be in some stress."

"But... Maybe I should..."

Interrupting her, Charlie said, "They left the outside camera on, but it will not work until the black hole has been trans versed. Then the EM machine will cut off, and the normal ship's functions will come back on again. Do not leave the ship for any reason. It will separate you from your body forever. Perhaps you would even lose your soul at this speed."

The warning wasn't necessary. She didn't plan on going outside. She watched him disappear through the wall. Her security was leaving. She felt very alone. She wanted to go with him, but she felt a need to stay and protect the bodies of her crew.

She floated around the room. The emergency life support system continued to function normally. She checked the others. They were breathing okay. Even the Reverend High Achiever

Kole was strapped in her chair. He seemed to be taking it. The acceleration continued to press them hard against the soft fabric. She could even feel the pressure pulling at her. It took a certain amount of effort to hold her position.

She looked at Judy. The tears, allowed to run, had left streaks on her cheeks. Moving in closer, she tried to give the body a hug. She did not know how in this state. She found herself covering her totally. Judy's body moved, her face smiled.

She picked up something more. Yes, Judy touched her. The sensation ran through her fabric. She gently pulled back. "Not now hon," she said easing herself away from the chair. She brought herself back to focus, but the feeling remained.

Then she picked it up. Something was watching her by the lift. Quickly turning, she saw a white cloud with a pink tinge coming through the walls. It wanted her! The emotion filled her 'Being'. It wanted her now! She looked around quickly. Trapped, the only walls to go through led to the outside. It was not a good option. She remembered Charlie's warning.

More of the White 'Being' poured into the room and began to fill it. "How big is this thing and how long have these people been harboring it?"

"I am God!" The 'Being' said, "We must become one before we pass through the 'Gate to Heaven'."

"I don't believe you are God! You look like a big spook to

me!" She couldn't believe she was talking to the 'Being'. She didn't quite understand how she did it. The thought of touching the 'Being' scared her.

"We must join now!" It insisted. "We must become one!"

It was not really speaking to her. It was more of an emotion she was picking up. Then the emotion was put into her words. These facts took only seconds. She remembered the 'Being' in the black pod telling her this. All this time she was backing more towards the bow of the ship. Now there was no more space to retreat to.

The 'Being' occupied most of the room. "No, it's floating filaments did," she thought. The condensed pinkish core, where the emotion was coming from, was two meters in diameter. The rest of the 'Being' was feeling the room and approaching her. A long wispy part of the 'Being' touched her fabric.

Immediately recoiling, she found herself going out the skin of the ship. She stopped abruptly. The scene in front of her became even more terrifying than one behind her. They were piercing the black hole. The event horizon became only a blur. She was forced back to the hull of the ship. She felt her essence spreading over the metal surface. She could not move finding herself becoming hypnotized by the slow whirling blackness in front of her. Lasting seconds, but her senses stretched it into a lifetime. In slow motion they blasted through the hole, and out into the blackness on the other side, or was it?

Leaving the whirling hole far behind, they were outstripping the dark purple cloud surrounding the ship. Only a few hundred meters of cloud remained, and this was quickly evaporating. A brilliant white background seeking entrance filled the void behind it.

She knew it wanted them. She could feel the pain of the dark purple mass dissolving into the white mass. It broke down the Purple 'Being'. The weaker lighter colors that made up the purple mass began to separate out. The light pink, yellow, darker red, then the orange and green separated. Finally, the remaining brilliant blue separated from the Dark Purple One becoming absorbed into the white substance.

Their speed left these colors far behind creating a brilliant rainbow tail spreading out in a fan shape behind them. Only straight ahead was the Purple One still intact. She was picking up overwhelming pain and depression from those behind. It was as though the 'Beings' that made up this Purple One were losing their souls in this white morass. It was a slow continuous pain. The white morass sought to dissolve them all! She seemed to be linked in with the feelings of this Purple One. She could barely stay focused.

It all seemed so clear to her. This large purple 'Being' was a completed meld of billions of other 'Beings'. All things in her universe were in the process of becoming or were a part of it. Now it was coming apart. These souls were being ripped away to be dissolved into the White morass in front of her.

The White 'Being' was more than white. She could see fragments of colors, red and yellow, floating through the morass, or was it the result of the 'Dark Purple One' breaking down. The White 'Being' was all on this side of the darkness. It was similar to the Purple Being's dark universe on the other side.

They were surviving, but the cost was enormous. The Purple One was actually sacrificing himself in huge amounts to give them the little success they were achieving. It was not going to be enough! Long before they came to a rest, and reversed the process, the white substance would eat its way through to them.

The Purple One was trying to stop their acceleration, but there was not enough of him left to be effective. Thinning to forty meters, the Purple One moved with them, but there was a limit to his strength. It had to be seconds before they broke through his protective shield. Then the white beast would attack them.

Awed, she could see clearer now that the dark fabric had faded. A sea of whiteness stretched out as far as she could see. It appeared smooth except for a small clump moving towards them. As it approached closer, it seemed to be darker. It was! The Purple One was heading toward it. His fabric was almost gone.

The clump became larger. "Yes, it's much larger!" It was not a clump, but a large round knot of energy the size of a large star. It was coal black, hard, and alive! She felt this deep inside. She also knew it had the density of a hundred universes. These thoughts were not hers. They were coming from somewhere.

It made an opening! "They were entering the Black 'Being'!" The enormous controlled presence of the compacted 'Being' overwhelmed her.

Suddenly the brilliant white morass was gone. Only the heavy blackness remained. She felt the pressure easing. The blackness was thinning out. They were still moving but continued to slow.

The sea of blackness allowed them movement, but there were walls. Yes, walls with a hardness way beyond anything she could comprehend extended beyond her senses. The 'Being' was actually growing larger. It changed its dense compact structure to this lighter substance. She was inside a large growing sphere. She also knew it could condense again crushing their fragile structure easily.

She picked up more. Everything became so clear, "This 'Being' used to be a universe. Yes, much bigger than ours. Now, after being consumed by a black hole, it had condensed down into this black sphere to survive the white morass outside. Even with this, the Black 'Being' became its victim. Slowly the white substance ate away at its black skin."

Was this Black 'Being' communicating with her? This information seemed to be flowing into her. No, it was the Dark Purple 'Being' trying to educate her on one level while it communicated with the Black One on another. She stopped trying to analyze the process and listened.

The Black 'Being' continued, "Yes, the filaments of yellow and red were part of White One's make up, but no central core or intelligent center existed. At least they have not found one yet. The swirling colors in the white fabric seemed to be the only collected portions.

It was this very fact that made the substance invulnerable. What do you attack? Where do you apply pressure? Surrounding and taking a chunk of white 'being', even with a color portion, did little except make us, the black condensed portion, more soluble to its constant caustic attack. Our only defense has been the tightness of our skin, but even this slowly dissolved. They will eventually absorb us totally.

We believe they have emotion and feelings, but communication is impossible when our barriers must remain impassable to survive. Yes, sacrifices have been made, but all have ended in disaster.

Yes, we have our successes. The darkness from which you come was one of them. Many have sacrificed themselves and will continue to do so to maintain it. It has allowed us to experiment. We have learned much."

Ana could see a dark barrier of extremely dense matter holding back the White One. Inside the softer fluid matter was almost empty allowing free movement of the huge purple entity (her universe filled with stars and galaxies).

"What you have learned will be shared by all. Your term, creating energy, was actually learning how to manipulate the white substance."

Ana could see the large spiral galaxies spinning in energy seemingly from somewhere beyond the darkness. "Galaxies were creating and condensing energy. There was no Big Bang! From the bloom of the black pod all things grew after the entity learned to create energy. Actually, it did not create energy, but drew it from this side of the black barrier."

The Black One continued without waiting for these concepts to take hold. "Learning to draw the white energy across our barriers was not all that impressive. The way you did it was different, but the important part of the project was your unique way of melding the pure strength, blackness, with the pure sensitive, whiteness. This has possibilities. We also thank you for your gift, though we almost lost it to the white substance."

Suddenly the conversation struck something deep. "Gift? What gift?" She asked.

"Why, your total project is on your space vehicle."

Yes, it suddenly became clear. It was like he pressed the right button. It opened waves of emotion and understanding. Each 'Being' behind her carried a pure form of the project. She remembered the book, 'The Creation of One,' the entities had melded into one being. This formed the basic structured blocks for the Dark Purple Being, the one creating our universe. These impressions began to flow through her.

The Black One ignored these feeling. This was all new to her, but he wasn't talking to her. This conversation continued with the Purple One.

"The ship will stay here representing your highest development," The Black One said. "Its integrity will be maintained by our energy."

Ana didn't have to be educated to understand The Black One wanted their Starship. She pulled back and was ready to object when the Black One stopped his dialog to the Purple One and focused on her feelings.

"No, you and your crew will be allowed to return, but your time is short. Already his purple fabric thins, and the black funnel closes. The white substance has never eaten so well. We do appreciate his sacrifice, and yes there is another in your blackness."

She began to feel the urgency of leaving. Her 'Being' picked up the distress in the Purple One. The conversation above her was already fading out. A dense noise had replaced the clear concepts of the moments before. Yes, the Purple One was communicating at a pace beyond her ability to understand, but she did pick up one emotion strong and clear. He wanted her to leave now! This emotion, consuming, forced her out of the linkage with the Black One.

8 The White 'Being'

Yes, Ana knew it was time. Turning inward, she slipped back through the skin of the ship. She noticed those in the chairs had moved. Their essences were returning. They had begun the process of focusing back into their reality. Though, the pinkish flowing energy in front of her was the most striking. It had condensed into a small core of spinning energy trying to protect itself.

Taking advantage of this, Ana quickly slipped by the whirling mass, dispersing herself through the far wall. The process was still not perfect and took her a moment to think of the whole wall before she could make the transition.

Behind her the spinning White Being slowed, then stopped. She felt it watching her. She wanted to move faster, but she was distracted. She felt herself ease through. She quickly moved to the deck and started her descent through it while the White Being floated above her.

She was picking up something from the White 'Being'. It was radiating a deep and profound emotion. She wanted to meld with her. It was actually pleading with her to do so.

Deciding she needed to set the right tone here, she allowed herself to link slightly, communicating with it. "No, she had no interest there. She was leaving and taking only her crew."

Immediately, Ana picked up deep emotions of desertion. "No," she continued, "You are supposed to stay here with the others. Only my crew will be allowed to leave. The Black One will see to your needs. You have nothing to fear."

Mentioning the Black One sent the White 'Being' into a visible breakdown. The 'Being' became erratic. She began moving in different directions at the same time to the point of almost dispersing herself.

Ana completed her descent moving up the hallway rapidly. She left the distraught White One behind. Staying in the hallway was easier than attempting the walls, but she knew she needed to descend two more levels to reach her body and safety. She felt once her essence was locked in and focused in the quote real reality, she would be able to block the White One. She must keep the 'Being' from touching her!

She looked back. She didn't see anything, and quickly spread herself out. She visualized the whole deck and began dropping through. Suddenly she heard a screeching noise. Thinking it was above her, she quickly dropped on through. The screeching increased. Behind her, coming fast was the White

Being in total panic.

Ana felt the emotions and the overwhelming desire to meld emitting from the 'Being' coming towards her. She turned racing up the hallway away from her body.

"I can't let her touch me," she yelled inside. Emotionally she was a mess too. In fact, she might encourage the meld if the White One touched her. How much resistance could she put up? Right now, she didn't want to test.

The White 'Being' probably picked this up. It could be what put her into such a frenzy. Something else bothered her. The 'Being' appeared to be pure. The others never did meld with her. Yes, the White Being made an imprint on them, but never the true meld it wanted. The joining of waves would have made them into a new 'Being'. They would be different, an accumulation of all their waves, and more.

This was not the pseudo meld a person has with another person's body wave during a sexual act. This was left behind when the person left his body or died. These thoughts hung over her in one emotion of fear. Amazed at herself, she could analyze this, simultaneously she felt the total emotion of fear.

It was only seconds before she was out of hall space. Trapped, the 'Being' would take her. Feeling defeated, she was about to turn and face it, when she felt a vent beside her.

"Yes!" She shouted. Flowing into it, she found herself going through a narrow tunnel downward.

At a sharp bend she stopped and began easing herself through the metal wall. "Think wall," she yelled. "Think wall, not the 'Being' behind you. Wall! Wall!" The screams behind her became louder.

The 'Being' was pleading with her, saying, "Meld! Meld! Please! We must meld now!"

These emotions were coming through, but the overall emotion of the 'Being's' panic screams drowned them out. The White 'Being' took the sharp corner, went screeching past, descending on down the metal duct.

Ana, finding herself in the open hallway, raced back towards her body. She knew it was on this level. She needed to transverse two more doors then she would be in her body. Feeling victorious, she started to smile until she heard the screeching behind her. The 'Being', picking up her scent, was coming back.

Ahead was the locker door. She did not have time to ease her way through. Picking up speed spreading herself, she smashed through the door. Not even slowing she ignored the pounding pain in her fabric and pushed into the second door. But her speed was too slow. She smashed hard into the metal airlock door. A part of her 'Being' had reached through, but the bulk of her was stuck in the door.

Pain consumed her 'Being' taking away all other thoughts. She tried to push the pain deeper, but her fear was controlling her. She could hear the screaming demon coming closer. She needed to clear her mind and move on through the door. Concentrating, she began to move the pain deeper into her fabric, but she was too late. The White One was here!

Passing through the first locker door easily, the White 'Being' attacked. She quickly moved her white essence over Ana's trapped 'Being'.

Unable to move, Ana felt the tingling fingers work their magic into the folds of her fabric. She felt herself wanting her. Huge amounts of energy deep inside were screaming to be released. Her emotions were slowly slipping out of her control.

She tried to close them off, but images flashed into her mind. Karl Haggen's, her stepfather's face came straight toward her. His eyes wanted her, but he was married to her mother. She was able to turn allowing him slide by.

She knew what was coming next. She turned and ran through the fog. "Yes, fog now," she thought, "She must escape before…Before…"

A soft voice called and followed her deeper into the mist. It was coming closer. She knew whom that voice belonged to. "No! I will not let it happen!" She yelled.

She ran faster and deeper, but the weak voice seeped through seeking her. "Please Ana, don't run from me. Please…Wait."

It was not fair to use her voice! It was not fair! The 'Being' found her weakness! She must shut her mind off! The 'Being' is…"No!" She shouted. "I must run, but what direction?" The soft voice, coming closer, was all around her. It came out of the fog, beautiful, desiring her.

"Ana, I am here!" The voice said. "Please, why do you run from me?"

She watched the pinkish white wisp of fabric extend from the arms and touch her. Not resisting, she allowed it to bring up her own desires.

She felt strange. A part of her resisted, but she knew it was only seconds before she took the fabric moving into her. She would meld and release the pent-up energy inside of her. But another part of her stood off to one side to watch. It knew it was the White One caressing her fabric, but she could do nothing about it. Then she noticed something deeper.

Dropping lower, she picked up more! "The pain was here!" The pounding pain she buried a moment before wanted to emerge. Concentrating, she brought it up. Her mind was in the middle. She felt her fabric giving in to the sensitive above, and she felt the pounding pain below. Suddenly she connected the two sending the throbbing pain to the surface. It smashed into the unprotected fabric of the White 'Being'.

The pain instantly filled the 'Being's' delicate fabric. Collapsing, the White 'Being' pulled back her prying fingers. She tried to roll into her protective whirling shield, but the pain was already inside. Hurting, the 'Being' did not understand the sudden rejection. She fell back into a mass of pulsating pain.

Suddenly freed, Ana spread herself out easing through the door. Seeing her body, she moved over it, but she was confused. How did she get into it before? She hugged it, but nothing happened. It felt foreign and alien. Her body didn't want her!

"No wait!" She said. "I must be doing something wrong." She stared at it a few seconds.

"Maybe if you lay down next to it, you could roll in." The thought came from somewhere inside.

Yes, she moved down beside it. Suddenly something hit her hard from the back and hung on. Instantly she knew who it was. Panicking, she went with the movement, continuing to roll into her body taking the attached White 'Being' with her.

Her body, not recognizing the intrusion, reacted violently inside the spacesuit. She knew it didn't want her! She tried to relax, but she felt the ugliness attached to her back. She didn't want that in her body, but it wasn't going to come off! She could feel its fear clinging desperately to her. A part of her wanted to go back out. It still desired the meld. Her emotions hung. Another part of her was ripped raw by the sudden departure the moment before. But the rational part of her controlled forcing her to relax.

The vibrations became less violent, allowing her to become more in sync with her body's wave. Slowly she settled down. She didn't dare move until the vibrations stopped all together.

Thinking she was in, she sat up. Her body didn't come with her, and the vibrations started. More, the returning throbbing pain was trying to keep her out of her body. "It must be the sensitive on my back," she thought. "It learns fast!"

Forcing herself, she dropped back into her body. "I must take it slower." She eased into the pain allowing it to move deeper inside. "Just the eyes," she thought. "Try just the eyes." They felt like someone had glued them shut. "They won't open!" She started to panic. "They won't open!"

Calming herself, she concentrated on moving her arms. They felt numb. She knew they moved, but she couldn't feel them. Her legs were the same. The blood supply from the acceleration had been pulled from the front portion of her body. In fact, her body had deteriorated badly since she left it. She could smell the stench. A part of her wanted to discard it, but she didn't dare. She refused to become a victim to the White 'Being' on her back.

Ignoring the repulsion, she began to move through the body. She filled the pores, then slowly she cycled herself through. Life began to come back. The heaviness of the movements became lighter.

She could function. Testing, she tried her left eye. Not pushing it, she eased it open, then the next one. Done, both of them were open, but she saw nothing but darkness. At first, she was frightened thinking she had gone blind until she remembered where she was.

Closing them, she saw the White One trying to hide from her inside. Enough was enough! Feeling the power beginning to build deep inside, she forced it toward the White One, and pushed. Immediately the 'Being' knew it had failed. It moved from her body floating out of the airlock. The window for melding was past.

Ana, relieved, continued to test her body until she had everything working. Suddenly she felt something pulling her. Thinking the White One had returned, she kicked with her free leg, sending her assailant back out of the open airlock.

"Airlock!" She thought. "I just kicked somebody!" Praying she didn't do any serious damage, she slipped out of her suit and crawled back into the locker room. She could see someone on the floor against the far door. It was Parker holding his stomach. He tried to stand.

"Didn't know you were all that angry?" Parker said under a tight lip.

"Sorry! Sorry! I thought you were some spook that has been chasing me."

"I yelled into your outside speaker!" Parker said in an irritated voice.

Remembering, she said, "Oh, sorry! I turned it off. I didn't hear you. Not that you didn't get what you deserve."

Parker, finally standing, asked, "You mean the crew?"

"What kind of person destroys the brain of his crewmates?"

"One trying to save them. I set up a blind to deceive the Reverend High Achiever."

"What do you mean, a blind?"

"Just that! He thinks they're converted, but they are only in a hypnotic trans-state."

"You can bring them out of it?"

"In a second."

"I'm not buying it, you tried to kill me!"

"No! No!" He replied apologetically. "There was something weird in you! I couldn't affect your wave. And yes, I almost took you too far trying, but it was to protect you, not hurt you. But…But how did you know."

Ana, changing the subject, "Can you get my crew down here?"

"And do what?"

"We're going back with the EM Unit."

"Then you haven't noticed, we're no longer attached."

Ana quickly looked out the airlock, but all she could see was the darkness. Then turning back to Parker, "We take the shuttle! Have Mr. Henderson disconnect the positive drive pods and put it on the shuttle. He should find them about mid ship on the skin somewhere."

"You out of your mind, woman? That shuttle can't survive the acceleration, and if it does, we're going to be left drifting in space. How are we going to survive with one week of supplies and three months from Alpha eleven? That is saying the shuttle can accelerate there."

"One step at a time, Doctor. Now, I would advise doing what you can to help in that direction. I do know time is short, so let's move it!"

He watched her going out the door. "Where are you heading?"

"To say goodbye and distract our benefactors for you. They may not agree with our leaving."

Parker nodded, lifted his wrist communicator.

Ana heard him give a command. She waited until he began instructing them to assemble in the locker room. Satisfied, she moved on up the hall. Instinctively she knew where she was going. Moving up one level, she turned to her left. Yes, she could feel them. Rounding the corner, she entered the open door of the huge bedroom.

The bed was gone. A large chair occupied the space with the Reverend High Achiever Kole sitting on it. The others stood on the side or behind him filling the room. In front of the chair laid the Reverend High Achiever Kenzie. He was curled up in a fetal position. Yes, they were expecting her.

The Reverend High Achiever Kole stood, walked towards her. "Come in, my dear, no one wishes you harm. Not even our Reverend Kenzie here."

Ana took a few more steps forward and stopped. She did not want to give up her escape route. "I think I'll stay here if it's all the same to you."

"Whatever pleases you, but be assured we will not harm you, or cause you to miss the EM unit going back."

"Then you know we're taking the EM unit, and leaving?"

"Yes, but you may not take any of our provisions. We will need them here until our true conversion is experienced."

"You mean none of you has been converted?" Ana asked her voice sounding surprised.

"We represent the rebel in our order. It was the reason they selected us for this one-way journey. It created an opportunity to rid the order of its discontents. You see we believed there was more. Some of the paranormal experiments were recorded. We researched and expanded their concepts until we evolved into this." He extended his arms out indicating those standing around him.

Ana, confused, "Sorry, all I see are you people."

"Aw yes, but what are we? You have met the Reverend Kenzie."

She looked down at the fetal position of Kenzie. He was

sucking his thumb.

"He was a little shaken up after his experience with you."

"Me?"

"Yes, the White One, or I might add, the purest form of a sensitive in existence on our side of the darkness."

"Why do I feel I was set up?"

"Sorry, my dear, but after Captain Craine's breakdown, we were desperate. Then when we read Doctor Parker's report on your experience with the Black Pod, we knew we had our problem solved. As it turned out we were right."

"I was lucky. It could very easily have gone the other way."

"No, my dear, you had already proven yourself to be more than capable."

"You still haven't answered my question. You seem capable of handling Kenzie here. Why did you need Captain Craine or me?"

"Because we were all forced out of our bodies during the extreme acceleration. I'm sure you experienced the persuasive abilities of the White One. We were all extremely vulnerable. We needed to remain pure for each of us carries a portion of the great conversion in our bodies. We will of course join later, probably many times, but then it will be monitored by many."

"Let me understand this. I was your decoy for the White

One."

"We had to make sure the White One remained pure. She represents the closes link to the white substance that occupies most of this side of the Black Barrier. This is a rare opportunity for the Black One outside."

"What if I had failed?"

"Then all of you would have stayed with us of course."

"I don't get it? Maybe me, since I would be contaminated, but why the others?"

The Reverend High Achiever smiled, "My dear, each of you can replace one of us."

Ana looked at him and slowly backed away. She could not say a word. Cords were being touched sending waves of emotion rippling through her.

Breaking into her thoughts, the High Achiever Cole said, "It is time for you to leave. If you stay longer, you will not be able to leave emotionally or physically. I may have told you too much already."

She nodded, backed further, and stumbled out the door. It was enough. The concepts made sense in the other focus, but in this one it only confused her. The simple philosophies drilled into her since childhood could not be ignored. Though if she were to hear them for the first time without prior conditioning she probably would have reacted the same.

Bodhi Two – Black Hole

9 The Return

The Passenger

Quickly Ana moved down the hall. Entered the lift, it seemed to be going slow. She knew it wasn't, but the urge to leave was building. They were dealing in minutes and precious few of them. Coming out of the lift, she took advantage of the low gravity, pulling herself faster through the hall. The thought of her out of body race renewed her fear intensifying her urge to move faster.

"They must leave! They must leave now!" This emotion burned in her head. She pulled herself harder towards the locker room and the airlock.

Parker had the room stacked to the ceiling with supplies. He was trying to push the animated suspension unit into the airlock, when Ana came in. "Where have you been? Could have used some help here."

"Where are the others?"

"On board putting the positive unit in. Should be about finished, but they left me with all of this."

"Leave it!" She ordered. "Pull that A.S. Unit out of there! We're getting out of here, now!"

"What? Leave all of this?"

"There is no time! Leave it or stay with it! We may not make it even now!" Not waiting for Parker to respond, she jerked the A.S. unit out of the airlock. She turned to see him staring at her. "Well?" She asked.

"What did they say to you?"

"Can we do this later, Parker?" She reached for her spacesuit and began putting it on.

"What's the hurry if we're going to die later anyway?"

"You rather die on this side of the Black Barrier and join the religious freaks above, or take your chances on the other side?"

"See your point," he started into his spacesuit.

Not waiting for him, she zipped up. Then through the suit's communicator, "If you're not on board in sixty seconds, you're staying!" She ducked her head and closed the airlock.

The walkway was still airless. It forced her to pull herself forward by using the handrails. Picking up speed, she reversed herself, using her feet against the shuttle to stop her momentum. It gave those inside a sharp shake. She didn't like doing it this way, but it saved her thirty seconds. She knew Parker would take longer.

Swinging into the airlock, she entered the shuttle. Everyone was busy. Mr. Henderson had all the panels off, and the wire-like filaments pulled out. Parts of a large box were scattered around the cabin. The four huge positive pods were being placed into position against the bulkhead. Lockers and chairs were pulled out to make room.

Ana zipped her suit down part way, surveyed the situation, then yelled, "Ready for lift off in thirty seconds!"

Henderson worked his head out of the mess below the front console. "You've got to be kidding."

"No!" She yelled. "We do it now or forget it!"

"But I'm not hooked into the panel yet!" Henderson protested.

"Forget the panel, just twist the filaments together where they are. We'll straighten them out on the other side."

"If they come loose, we may not get there."

"It's either that or not try. Our ticket home is leaving now!"

"See your point, Judy, are you about done with your end?"

From the other side of the shuttle a voice yelled out from behind the locker. "The positive unit is in place, but not secured well."

"It will have to do. Our Captain says we lift off in what, twenty seconds?"

Ana not responding took the command chair and strapped in. She flipped a few switches and lit up the cabin and the blackness outside.

George came up fast from below the floor panel, yelling, "Wait! It's hot down here!"

"I said thirty seconds! I meant thirty seconds! Now you have ten!"

The outside airlock opened, and Parker stumbled in. Before he could close the hatch, the shuttle lifted off the flight deck with the Doctor's one leg hanging outside. He screamed over his communicator, "I told you I'm no space jockey! Can't you let me get the rest of my body inside?"

Ana, while turning the craft, yelled back, "Just move it Parker, or you're going to be stuck there during the acceleration."

"Are you trying to kill me?"

"The thought crossed my mind."

The outside bay door opened, and the small craft moved out into the darkness.

Judy took her position on the left side of Ana. She looked outside. "It feels so cold! Do we really become that?"

"It's only a phase. The darkness sensitivity part will be released again when it can survive. Now it would be dissolved into the white fabric outside."

"I think I like our side."

Ana nodded. She heard Parker making his way from the airlock. He started to take off his suit, when she yelled, "You better leave it on. The rest of you get yours on. You too, Judy! I'm not sure how well the shuttle will take the EM docking let alone the acceleration."

Henderson, way ahead of Judy, had his on, and took her position. "Sensors are picking up the EM unit. Twenty degrees starboard," he said, "We're almost on top of it, but I can't see a thing. Maybe you better slow. We don't want to ram it."

Ana, not responding, turned the craft slightly to line up with the sensors.

Henderson looked at her a second, then stared out into the cold darkness. "I…I think we should approach it slower, ma'am."

Ana was locked in a hypnotic trance. Her eyes were open, but she was not really seeing anything. Her hands moved the controls and responded perfectly with the sensors.

Henderson, nervous at first, started to raise his voice to say more, but changed his mind. His fear prevailed. He did not want to break whatever she was linked with.

All of them in the cabin picked up his fear becoming silent. They watched her maneuver the craft. On full acceleration it moved quickly through the blackness. Any moment they expected their tiny vessel to smash into the starship or the EM unit.

Suddenly Ana broke the silence. In low monotone voice, she said, "Be ready to activate the positive unit in ten seconds, acceleration in fifteen!"

Everyone strapped in quickly except Henderson. He had ducked under the console. His fingers were ready to bring the two filaments together.

Ana was counting. "Four, three, two, now, Mr. Henderson." Ana brought the thrusters controls down hard. It reversed the engines braking the craft.

Henderson struggled from below the console to get back in his chair. "I hope you got it right, ma'am. That splice welded itself closed. There won't be a second try." He just reached his chair, when he found himself slammed against it. There was no loud noise. Only the silent vibration and acceleration was felt.

Slowly Henderson reached up, closed his head plate, then he allowed his heavy arm to collapse in the chair. He looked at Ana beside him. Her suit was in place, but she was staring straight ahead. Following her gaze, he saw the pinhole of light becoming larger. Then suddenly a brilliant flash of white light forced him to close his eyes. Yes, she was good.

Ana, even with all of her light filters down, still had to squint her eyes to see. Her filters were made to take direct sunlight, but this seemed brighter. Maybe her eyes needed to readjust from the darkness, but she did not see any purple fabric. She knew some of the Purple One was with them, but it must be very thin here.

It would not be protecting them. In fact, it was as helpless as they were. They needed more bulk. They needed it fast. They were moving through the pure white substance. Only their speed prevented more of an attack, but she could feel the craft coming apart.

The 'Being' was looking for weaknesses. She knew it would find them. The shuttle wasn't made for taking this stress. She could feel the metal buckling. Suddenly the landing gear ripped free tearing a small hole in the belly of the craft.

At normal speed this would not happen, but accelerating through any substance, no matter how thin, created a drag. This would build the faster they accelerated. She was hearing this from someone. She felt it was the Purple One.

They were hurting the white substance too. She could feel its pain. Strange, she didn't notice this feeling earlier.

"They want to attach themselves and meld with the shuttle. They want to become one. The craft is an irritant in their

'Being'."

Where was she getting this information? Turning her head slowly, she saw a whitish cloud floating in the cabin. Looking down, she became aware of the twelve-centimeter hole made by the sheared landing gear.

Knowing there was only seconds before the real acceleration hit and drove her from her body. She unbuckled her belt. Suddenly she found herself against the locker door with her back wanting to press on through it. She could feel the pain and knew she had done something bad to herself. Pushing the pain deeper, she slowly eased her left arm into the locker. She took out an eighteen-centimeter repair plate, activated it, and threw it over the hole.

Immediately the metal plastic material fused itself to the shuttle's skin closing off the hole. She had no idea what got in, but she had to get back to her seat. She could see the bulk of the purple fabric coming up.

Pulling hard, she noticed the craft was slowing. It allowed her to make progress. Yes, she had hurt herself badly. The Black One must have propelled them toward the greater bulk of the Purple One. Even now she was not sure it would be enough. She found her seat strapping herself in.

The Purple One was seeking them. She felt it drive off the white substance and surround their craft. Her senses picked this up, but there was no time to think about it. The sling shot was in effect. More of the Purple Fabric gathered behind them filtering out the bright light. She didn't need her dark filters, but she couldn't do anything about it. The acceleration was slow at first, but it quickly picked up speed. It flung them toward the closing black hole. She could see the Purple Fabric fighting to keep it open.

Suddenly she was ripped from her body. She found herself floating toward the back of the cabin. She struggled to keep from going out the shuttle's skin. She knew she was going to. She felt herself spreading out. She started to panic. She would be left on this side of the black hole! Worse, she would be absorbed by the white substance! Only her empty body would make it through!

"Join us!" A voice said.

Quickly looking around, she saw Charlie clinging to a mass of colors.

"Hurry, before you are cast adrift. They do not know how to transverse walls yet. Their fear prevents them. They make good anchors. They are not like you or me."

Ana, not having to be told twice, flung herself at them. Her fear joined theirs. Quickly the fear in the group intensified. "No, they will not be going through any walls," she thought.

Ana felt something strange with them. She didn't want to dislodge it. She knew they all would suffer especially Charlie and her. She looked at the limp bodies in the flight chairs. They were being pushed against the fabric giving each a distorted look. All of them appeared the same except George. Somehow his body felt different.

She wanted to check the body closer, but the view screen showed them approaching the black hole rapidly. They were still accelerating. She could see how much smaller it was. Maybe it was the direction, she thought. It had another event horizon extending out from it, but it didn't seem as large. In fact, it was closing in on them as they approach it.

Then it quickly came in behind them and pushed. They were being sucked through and pushed simultaneously. It happened so fast, she wasn't sure! The whole structure was collapsing around them.

The screen automatically switched to the aft camera. It showed a huge mass of very dark energy coming towards them. In slow motion it became larger. The dark mass, spreading outward, appeared to be engulfing them, but this was only an illusion. Whole galaxies and their stars were being absorbed in the consuming black mass. As if by magic, they disappeared. She knew of the sacrifices taking place. She heard Charlie behind her.

"He is closing off the black hole. This part of his fabric will require many eons to repair itself." He picked up her fear. "Do not worry, he will not let anything happen to his prize."

Ana turned. She didn't quite understand, but she knew the word 'prize' carried with it some deep emotions involving her. She wanted to question him, but the acceleration suddenly began to slow. The others, feeling better, were seeking their bodies.

She watched their attached stems pull their essence back. They sucked their pure light colors back into their lifeless forms. "Yes, they do carry the pure ones for the Creation of One," she thought. "Interesting, she never knew this before. Even George, the purest of them all, carried the white sensitive. She never suspected this of him."

"Beautiful, isn't she?" A voice said.

"Huh?" Turning, she saw a dull blue mass floating behind her. He was not dense. She would not see him at all except for her out of body state. "Who…Who are you?"

"You call me George."

Turning back to the bodies quickly, she saw the last of the white essence seeping into George's body in the space chair. "If that's George, who are you?" She asked. Becoming alarmed, she didn't like what she was feeling.

"No, I'm here! I let her have my body."

"Where did she come from?"

"I believe from the hole in the deck before you repaired it. She wanted to meld with me, but she felt Alien. To protect the rest of you in the circle, I agreed to let her have my body to meld with."

"But George, what about you? That's your body!"

"Let her have it! The Greater Part of me desires this. She already has my memories. There shouldn't be any problems."

"You're crazy! She'll want to meld with everything in sight."

"Yes, but in my body, her essence will remain pure. It's the safest place for her. She gets what she wants, but only the body will be affected."

"The imprint, George! The imprint!"

"Yes, but not permanent. It will make her ready for the blending of the waves later. My Greater Part says she is the non-attenuated source of the essence in Parker. Sort of a flip flop in time. Interesting isn't it."

She didn't know what he was talking about, "Blending waves." Emotions deep inside of her began to stir. "No," she thought, "Not now." Then thinking of George, she said softly, "You didn't answer my question. What about you?"

"I'll stay with the vessel awhile, if that's all right with you."

"It's fine with me, but she may seek you out. How will you control her?"

"By threatening to take my body back. I think she will be fascinated by it for a while. But yes, I will have to leave you. This is the danger."

Ana began to feel a tug from her own body. It wanted her back. Looking that direction, she saw Mr. Henderson and the doctor. They were zipping open her suit to revive her. "Got to go," she said. "I don't like this! I think you've set a sex maniac loose on my ship."

"Shuttle, ma'am!" He reminded her. "Shuttle!"

10 Collapsing Worm Hole

Ana smiled inside, but before she could answer, she felt her essence being sucked back toward her body. Parker had administered a stimulant. The drug was controlling. She found herself looking through moist eyelids. She saw Parker looking down at her.

"Decided to come back to the living?" Parker asked.

"Not quite yet, a moment longer would have been appreciated."

"Hmm, at least your foot isn't hanging out the door."

"Okay, we're even Parker!" She started to sit up when she felt a sharp pain in her back. "Can't move," she said, "Give me a second."

Doctor Parker eased her out of her spacesuit. In the free fall he could do it without exerting pressure. He looked at her back. "You've got a nasty cut here, and a bruise the size of a small melon."

"Just fix it, Parker!"

"Yes ma'am! You may not like it." He reached for his kit taking out the closing elastic bandage. It sealed itself to both sides of the wound. In seconds it closed neatly. "That will do the exposure. Your body will have to do the bruise."

"We haven't come all that far, have we, Parker?"

"Just be thankful we have anesthetic."

He started to reach for it, when she forced herself up. "No, I prefer the pain. It will keep me awake." She didn't tell him she needed it to concentrate on this reality. Already she was feeling herself drifting back inside when the pain brought her back.

Then looking at Mr. Henderson, she said, "Better get this ship back together. See what damage we've sustained."

"Yes ma'am!" He turned and started pulling out the panels. "Come on Parker, you got two hands. The wounded here don't want your help anyway. Maybe you can be more useful with me."

Ana noted the sarcasm, but her mind was on Judy floating back toward George in the aft part of the shuttle. Her eyes were looking at him in a furlong way. "Judy!" She snapped, "Up here with me!"

Judy turned with a wounded look. George gave her a curt stare then he quickly dropped it.

"That's good thinking, George," Ana said. "You leave my officer alone! You got that?"

George shrugged his shoulders, turned, and started peeling back the wall covering.

Mr. Henderson looked up, "I think that's assuming a lot, ma'am."

"He knows what I mean!" Ana snapped back.

"Yes ma'am!"

Ana was surprised at herself. Was she trying to protect Judy, or was there a selfish motive here? She didn't like it. Yes, that was all. She didn't like it and suppressed her displeasure. Let them think what they wished.

Judy, sitting beside her, whispered, "Sorry, thanks, I didn't know what came over me. He…He."

"It's okay. We can all forget it. Just keep away from him. Now check the long-range scan. See if you can pick up anything. I think we're drifting. The stars seem to be standing still."

Judy pressed the key board starting the transponder. Then she brought the overhead screen into the long-range scanner.

Ana started to turn away when the long-range scanner pinged. Whirling back, she said, "Something's out there, Mr. Henderson, do we have power?"

"In five minutes, some of these filaments are burnt to a crisp. We are lucky the EM unit stayed on."

"Make it two, Judy, are we on course?"

"We were! Now we're veering off."

"Mr. Henderson, I need something now. At this speed, we'll never get it again."

"I can give you a five second burst. Then we're going to be down for thirty minutes."

"Say when!"

"Anytime!"

Ana pushed the thruster lever on the console top. The shuttle came alive, but only for the five seconds. "How's that, Judy?"

"It…It seems to be okay. Hard to tell yet."

Ana checked, "Better! We should fall in their laps if we don't run over them first. Any idea how fast we're going George?"

George tried to put a fix on the stars, but he was not used to stars moving on him and became increasing frustrated. "Can't say…We're slowing though. Fast!"

The doctor stumbled forward. "I wouldn't be all that confident. There is no telling what that is? We don't even know where we are for-god-sake."

Ana, smiling, said, "We're where the Purple One wants us. We're in his fabric, remember?"

"Talk about spooks," Parker said, "Maybe we ought to try that psych tank again."

"Why, because I admit we're in something that thinks."

"I mean if you want to stay a Star Fleet Captain, you better think of another story. All of you," he said harshly, "And you better agree on it. Even let me put you in the psych tank at the first chance to confirm it."

"We see your point, Parker," she said, "Okay, we leave out the spook stuff and stay with the facts. Let them figure it out. They wouldn't let us bring the ship back. So, we rigged the shuttle and left with the EM unit. Good enough, Parker?"

"If you don't elaborate on it."

Judy broke in, "I think I have a fix. The signal is a space station."

Parker responding, "Probably Alpha Eleven."

"No…No…Its Alpha Twelve Station!"

"Alpha Twelve!" Ana said. She reached for her communicator tapping in the prefix code. "Alpha Twelve! Alpha Twelve!"

Over the screen a fuzzy picture of Mr. Monzor took form. His voice barely audible, "Identify yourself. I know you are not a

Starship."

"Monzor, this is Captain Mc Clure. You survived the EM blast. How about my crew?"

Monzor, responding, "We're picking up static! Is that you in the EM Unit?"

"Only the shuttle. The ship is gone."

"Monzor, with a desperate look on his face, said, "Do not approach closer! Do not approach closer! Your vessel is disrupting our circuits! We will destroy…"

The picture and the voice faded.

Ana tried to bring back the picture, and yelled, "Monzor! Monzor!" Nothing, she gave up, and turned to Mr. Henderson. "What does he mean, we're disrupting his circuits?"

"What do you think has been breaking us?"

"Friction, after the EM Unit turned off."

"No ma'am, not friction. We would still be way past light speed."

"Okay, give!"

"Electrons ma'am, the worm hole collapsed in front of us. We've been pushing our way through a collapsed hole full of electrons. It's slowing us, but not as fast as we accelerated. That's why we don't feel it as much, but can you imagine what we are pushing out in front of us. It has to be affecting them."

"But I thought the EM ship destroyed them along with our ship. Where did they come from?"

"I don't know, maybe they built another one. You know, the old theory of time."

"Not buying it, that was Monzor on the screen. It has to be the original."

"I guess we will have to ask them if they let us approach."

Judy, breaking in, said, "I have a second ping. This one is moving toward us."

Ana looked over at the long-range screen, "It could be our ship."

Parker interjecting, "Yes, with orders to destroy us."

"No, that's our people," Ana said turning toward him.

Parker shook his head. "No matter, listen to what Monzor said. They plan to destroy us."

Ana turned to Judy. "Turn that transponder off!"

"Yes ma'am!"

Mr. Henderson crawled out. "You have power now, Captain. Didn't do as much damage as I figured, but don't rely on them not finding us. I'm sure we light up their screen well with our electron wave."

"Can we brake faster, Henderson?"

"No, and I wouldn't advise doing so if we could. This is only a shuttle, not a spaceship."

Ana turned to George. "Did you get a fix yet?"

"I...I think so."

"Can you estimate our speed?"

"Maybe half the speed of light...I'm guessing, but looks like we're going to stop," he said hesitating a second, "Right where the pinging is coming from."

"Convenient!" Ana said. "Tell me that wasn't planned."

"Yes, with a proton bomb to meet us," Parker put in.

"I'm aware of the welcome, Doctor. What would happen if we broke out of the collapsed worm hole early? Can we slow ourselves down enough with our own engines?"

Mr. Henderson, calculating, replied, "How much fuel do you want to expend?"

"About half! We'll need maximum power."

Using the computer, Mr. Henderson came up with it. "Six Minutes ma'am. Six minutes of burn thirty seconds from the end of the EM braking. That's the best I can do. I wouldn't advise going sooner."

"How long before end of braking?"

"Two minutes and counting!"

"Okay everyone, strap in. This could be a hard one." She pulled herself back to her chair. Her hand felt the power lever. Turning back to Mr. Henderson, "Ready to cut the positive link?"

Mr. Henderson took a pair of insulated cutters. He placed the two filaments in them. "Ready!"

"We'll go to eighty seconds, Mr. Henderson. Coming up! Four! Three! Two! Cut!" Ana pulled the power lever. The shuttle, free of the EM unit, took a ninety-degree angle route through the closed worm hole.

Suddenly the shuttle's circuits flashed and died, but their momentum carried them on through the mass of electrons. Fire ignited, Mr. Henderson immediately pulled the lever above him to activate the fire extinguisher. The cabin was sucked free of oxygen. The fire went out. Then thirty seconds later the oxygen returned for the occupants to breathe. It was a practiced procedure. They all expected it.

Ana looked at Mr. Henderson, "How long on the repairs?"

"Didn't know you planned on crossing the electron current. We're lucky we didn't get ripped apart."

"I was wondering that myself. We must have found a rift in the current."

"Look ma'am, you've had more than your share of luck. I hope we don't continue to push it."

"Sorry, Mr. Henderson, I didn't have time for a discussion. How bad?"

Mr. Henderson checked under the console. "Looks like all the circuits are gone."

"Manual?"

"Everything manual."

"Okay Mr. Henderson, the engines," she said. "George, take a fix as soon as you can. I want to know where we are. I don't trust those pings. Back to basics, everyone in suits, but not zipped up. Have no idea how the oxygen cleaner will work. Parker, it's your job to tell us when to zip. Judy, go to emergency power on the outside camera."

Judy flipped the controls, but nothing happened. "Can't ma'am, the circuits have been damaged."

"Then I'll be in the airlock." Ana said zipping up her suit. She climbed into the airlock, hand sealed it, and peered out into the starlit darkness.

She checked her communicator. "Mr. Henderson, give the port a two second slow burn. I want to see the EM Unit."

Immediately the craft turned quietly in the airless blackness. "Brake it, Mr. Henderson! We've lost the worm hole!" She heard Henderson's voice.

"Is it leaving us?" He asked.

"No! We're not slowing!" Ana said, "The EM Unit is back in the electron cloud somewhere. Good thing we got out when we did. Nothing is going to leave that cloud until it moves on. It's expanding toward us, but we're outdistancing it. It was the space station all right! I can see it! The cloud is going to hit it!"

Mr. Henderson placed his fingers over the manual control, "When do you want the six-minute burn?"

"After the electron wave takes out their sensors. We need to put a little distance from this wave. There goes their power. The wave has them. Gees, there's fires everywhere! Parts of it are exploding! It's gone! Can't see more, they're buried in the cloud mass. We need to check for survivors."

"We better survive ourselves first, Captain!" Parker said.

"I'm aware! You may hit the power now, Mr. Henderson!"

The shuttle at full thrusters began slowing them.

Ana, after five and a half minutes, said, "Cut slightly on the starboard side. Let's make the last thirty seconds a loop. I want to be heading back toward the space station. George, give us a bearing to bring us into a wide orbit."

George, sitting in his corner, was looking out into the darkness, he had not moved. The 'Being' inside of him had never seen this much darkness before. Unable to move, "I...I am having trouble...The..."

"Just a guess, George. We can adjust later."

"Cutting the burn in ten seconds, and counting," Henderson said. He slowly tightens his grip. "Five, four, three, two, cutting!"

"Okay George, where are we?"

"I…I can't look anymore!"

"George take your time."

"I can't see…My eyes are blurring…I…"

"Judy, move him out of there and do it!"

"I can't! He has this weird look on his face. I think he's in a state of shock! He's about to explode!"

"Doctor, take the young man down. We need that bearing now!"

Parker quickly shot George with a hypo when he lunged for Judy. Falling past her, he flipped over, and floated to the other side of the cabin. He hit the bulkhead with his feet.

Parker reporting, "He's out for thirty minutes. I have no idea what set him off."

"Just keep him down!" Ana said, "Judy, if you please!"

Judy, stepping by George, tried to take the star bearing. "Not sure of this,' she said, "This is not my…"

Interrupting, "Mr. Henderson, give her a hand."

Mr. Henderson came out of his position under the console. "Let's see it, Judy!"

"I think we're a long way off." Her voice saying, she was about to cry.

Mr. Henderson, checking, said, "You might as well come in, ma'am. You won't be seeing it for a while, saying we have enough fuel to burn when we reach it."

"What's our speed?"

"Normal, but we're spewing fuel if this gauge is right."

"Assuming they are, did you close off?"

"Thought I did, but manual is always a guess, checking again." He ducked back under the console.

"Anytime Mr. Henderson?"

Coming back up, Mr. Henderson ripped out the port panel, and stared at the fuel release valve. "It's stuck, ma'am! Use the fuel now or forget it on the port side. We'll lose it all in six minutes."

"Give us a two-minute burn," Ana said, "Then try closing it off again!"

Mr. Henderson leaped back under the console and spliced the filaments. The craft accelerated back toward the space station.

Ana, coming out of the airlock, took a long metal tool from the wall. She pulled herself up beside the valve. "Parker!" She yelled, "Hold me! Let's see if this works!"

Parker pushed himself back and held her waist. He tried to brace himself against the bulkhead. When she swung the metal handle, the blow sent them both into the opposite wall.

The doctor, protecting himself, allowed Ana to take the hardest hit. Her back met the open bulkhead. The sharp rib structure found her huge bruise, and sent pain screaming through her body. Nature taking its course, she passed out, and left her limp body floating in the cabin.

Running from the pain, Ana found herself out of her body. Stopping, she looked back at Parker. He was easing her body part way out of her spacesuit. She watched him closing the wound. It was bigger after being ripped on the sharp bulkhead.

Mr. Henderson worked on her suit. He patched the hole and shook his head. Concentrating on them, she did not notice someone else coming up beside her. "Hope you didn't hurt yourself badly."

Whirling, she saw a dull blue mist floating four feet off the deck. Then she remembered. "George?" She asked.

"Yes ma'am. Sorry about my replacement. I wouldn't put much stress on her. She will fold again. I think it's the darkness upsetting her."

"Sometimes it cannot be helped."

"I did check your position for you. About three hours from Star Base Twelve on your present heading, saying it still has the same orbit."

"I can count on that?"

"You have time. I know you will check it out. I didn't want to worry you while you are out of your body. By the way, I wouldn't stay too long. The White One would much rather have your body."

"Where is she now?"

"Hiding up in the aft glow light scared, she's waiting for a comforting hand."

"And you?"

"Not giving it to her. I know where it leads."

Ana started back toward her body, "Guess it's time to bare the pain."

"Oh, the electron wave from the closed wormhole should reach you soon. You might want to prepare for it."

"Ana turned, "Where did you get that information?"

"From some guy named Charlie," he said, "Nice chap!"

"Yeah, I bet!" She rolled back into her body and fought the pain trying to push her out. She concentrated until she could focus on Parker's face. Then quickly she pushed him away to avoid the hurt look on his face. "Next time I'll get someone who will protect my back!"

The anger brought her back quicker. She reached out and pulled herself forward. The sudden pain told her it was a bad idea. It almost pushed her out again. She let Parker apologetically help her to her space chair.

He strapped her in, "Sorry ma'am…I couldn't hold you."

Mr. Henderson, coming to help, smiled. "You have the valve closed. All it took was a bigger hammer."

She ignored him, lifted her head, shouting, "Everyone into their chairs! Judy, strap George in!"

Parker pushed her back down. "You may want to stay put yourself for a while. That wound will open up again."

"It will have to wait. Now strap yourself in." She pushed his hands away. She looked at Mr. Henderson helping Judy secure George. "Mr. Henderson, let her finish. Set a course for 90 by 90 starboard and give us a three-minute burn."

Henderson set the course in and pulled himself back under the console. "What are we running from, ma'am?"

"The electron wave from the worm hole, our little maneuver put us ahead of it, but now it's our turn."

Mr. Henderson hit the power. The shuttle accelerated. It forced Parker and Judy to hold themselves in. After three minutes the acceleration stopped. They all started to remove their straps, thinking they would be missed, when the craft began to tumble.

Ana shouted at Mr. Henderson, "Another burn to stabilize!"

The craft engines kicked in. Immediately the tumbling stopped, and the craft leveled out.

Ana tried to pick up something on the view screen, but everything was a haze. "How many minutes of fuel do we have left?"

"Three minutes on the starboard side," Mr. Henderson yelled back. "We dumped or burned most of the port side when the value froze."

"Better leave two for maneuvering later."

"We may tumble again."

"We'll have to risk it. Keep us on a heading ninety degrees to the electron wave."

Mr. Henderson cut the engines after two minutes and allowed the craft to drift. There was no tumbling. Only the silence remained. He looked at Ana. "Could be out of it."

"Then turn us back on course."

Immediately Mr. Henderson, using the impulse button, edged the shuttle around. "Do we have a course, ma'am?"

"We do if someone can find that space station."

Judy worked the long-range scanner, "It's not working. Maybe the fire damaged it."

Mr. Henderson pulled himself over to the scanner. "The overload kicked in. The scanner's okay, only the filaments burned. Have it fixed in a second," he said, "There, try it now!"

Judy began working the scanner. "Picking up two objects. One way off to our portside. The other is on our heading."

"Any size differences?"

"Mass about the same."

Mr. Henderson, from below the console, said, "We better stay on our present heading until I can move some of this fuel to the port tank. We don't need to waste it with a wide turn."

"What's your best guess, Mr. Henderson? I don't think we can change our minds later with only one minute of burn left."

"Less, we just lost some in the turn, and with the exchange. I say stay on course. We can't afford a change."

Parker, not liking the decision, "And if it's the wrong one, like the spaceship?"

Mr. Henderson coming up from below, said, "It better be the Starship. The space station blew, remember?"

Parker, not giving in, "It has survival supplies there and maybe some fuel."

"He has a point, ma'am!"

Ana was not hearing him. She was barely hanging on. The waves of pain began to drive her out. In the background she heard Judy's voice. She was yelling at Parker to help her. She felt his hands touching her. Someone was looking at her open wound.

"It's open again and seeping badly. Her suit is wet with blood." The person cleaning her up was angry with someone.

Her mind shut it out and shifted to her parents. Her father was leaving them. She was hugging him outside the tube pleading for him not to leave. She felt her mother reaching over her and holding him close. He wasn't coming back. He broke their hold on him and boarded the tube. Her tears were flowing as she watched him leave.

11 The EM Unit

She knew she had to come back. Concentrating, she forced her way through the haze. She heard Parker talking.

"She's coming back. Two hours," Parker repeated, "She's coming back, but I think she's had all she can take. Maybe you better decide."

"Decide what?" She said fighting back the pain. She looked up at the three of them. "Decide what?"

"We have the object on the screen with the long-range camera. It's…It's the EM Unit." Parker said holding her down. He did not want his patient to move. "Mr. Henderson has it working, but you're not going anywhere!"

Turning her head slightly, she saw a fuzzy ball on the screen with something plugging up the middle. "What's that inside?"

Mr. Henderson squinting, "Looks like a spaceship. Could be ours."

"What's our heading?"

"Dead center!"

"Then cut all power! Even the lights!"

Suddenly George screamed and passed out in his chair.

Parker pulled himself that direction while Mr. Henderson cut the emergency power. "What's wrong with him?"

"Put a glow in locker three, and close the door," Ana said.

Parker looked at her in a weird way, but he did it. "I think you've lost your mind completely this time, ma'am!"

"Just do it Parker, and then secure George. He won't be coming around for a while. She released her straps and moved her arm. It felt better. What did you do, Parker?"

Parker, working with George, "I anesthetized it like I should have done earlier. You take it easy. No sudden movements. I don't think I can close that a third time."

She gave him hard stare. Then she moved over to the view screen. Judy gave her room and helped her to sit. Now, that they were closer. They could plainly see the EM Unit and the Starship.

"Is it our ship?" Judy asked.

Mr. Henderson behind her, said, "Yes, but it's not attached. It can't move it! Look, see how uneven the space is between the ship and the EM Unit."

"Then why is it there?"

"Don't know ma'am!"

Judy, pointing, said, "Look, the bay door is opening. Something is coming out."

Mr. Henderson, squinting, "Looks like the Beta shuttle. Maybe we should bring up the power now while the bay door is open, ma'am."

"No, let the shuttle pass. I don't want them to see us. We will wait until the EM Unit blocks their sensors. Then hit the power."

"But the bay door…It will close."

"Didn't plan on going in that way anyway."

The shuttle moved behind the EM Unit. Ana pulled herself back to her chair, "Anything work yet, Mr. Henderson?"

"The thrusters, you have about thirty seconds of burn in each engine."

"Hang on!" She pulled the lever to the back thruster for ten seconds, and the craft stopped. After a few short bursts she had the shuttle beside the spacecraft.

"Now what?" Mr. Henderson asked and disengaged his

straps.

Ana moved off her seat slowly, "We're going out! Parker, stay with George and the shuttle. When the bay door opens, take her in and dock. I wouldn't waste any time. You don't have the fuel. Mr. Henderson, go through the aft airlock and head for the engine compartment. Judy, come with me, we'll take over the Bridge." She pulled herself toward the airlock. "Blaster on stun," she said over her shoulder. "These are our people. Be sure your lifeline is attached before leaving the shuttle. We don't need an emergency here."

Mr. Henderson, working his suit on, asked, "What makes you think they are going to let us takeover?"

Parker, not liking his patient risking herself again, asked, "Yes, I would like an answer to that myself?"

Ana, turning, her voice was even and deliberate. "Where do you think that shuttle is going?"

Mr. Henderson, puzzled, "The space station probably."

"Space station exactly! A blown out one!"

Parker, picking it up, "To get survival supplies like we should have done."

"Right then wrong! The clue here is the EM Unit. Why is my Starship laying inside the EM Unit? It can't move it."

Judy, understanding first, "They're going to blow it up!"

"Exactly! No evidence! No explanations needed!"

Mr. Henderson, about to zip up, asked, "Then who is in the Beta shuttle?"

"The one setting this up. Monzor, or maybe our neurotic Captain Craine. We'll find out once we're inside."

Parker, interjecting, "I'd say Craine! Monzor doesn't have the personality for it."

"Good guess! Remember, Parker, play dead out here. We need surprise inside to have even a slight chance of pulling this off."

"They probably already know we're here," Parker said.

"Perhaps not, they would think our earlier burn was the Beta shuttle leaving, but now they would know for sure. Okay, Mr. Henderson first. Attach your line, no communication through the spacesuits. They can pick it up. Any questions before we leave?"

Mr. Henderson entered the airlock, "What am I doing once I secure the engine space?"

"Look for the explosive device. It has to be something big to take out the EM Unit too."

"Then I would look in the proton armory first and the fuel tank second."

"Okay, then Judy, you're with Mr. Henderson. Shed your

suit once inside," she continued, "Look below the plates above the fuel tanks."

"What am I looking for?" She asked.

"Anything out of place! Okay, everything set? Remember, Parker, when I have the bay door open, take her in. We may have to move fast. When you come inside, bring the positive units here with you. We may want to move the EM Unit too. Is that okay, Mr. Henderson?"

Mr. Henderson nodded while he finished zipping up. He closed the airlock. Outside he attached his life line and waited for Judy. In seconds she emerged. Then behind her was Ana. The two of them kicked off from the shuttle moving toward the spaceship. When they hit, Ana released their life line. When they attached themselves to the ship, she kicked off.

Once she was sure of her direction, she released the line from her suit, allowing herself to drift toward the ship. Immediately upon reaching the ship, she reached for the handhold. Fewer things hung out in the forward section, making this procedure difficult.

She hit the airlock square on. She started to bounce out when her hand caught the outside lever. It stopped her momentarily, but it cost her. She could feel the wound bleeding again.

Ignoring it, she opened the airlock and climbed in. "They're going to know someone went through the airlock," she thought.

She pushed the other door open and slipped out of her suit. She hid it in a locker. "No since in making it easy," she thought.

Taking out her blaster, she entered the hall. Up three levels was her destination. The lift was faster, but it was not as quiet. It felt good to walk. Her muscles needed to readjust. They wobbled at first, but she learned quickly. In seconds she was running up the hall in half gravity.

Something inside told her she didn't have time to be secretive. Opting for the lift, she turned left, entering the open door. Going up, she could feel her heart pounding. Weird, she wondered where all the people were? There should have been some movement on the lower deck, but there was nothing. She could feel the silence. It was like she was on a dead ship.

Pointing her blaster, the door opened. She leaped out in a defensive position, but there was no one to shoot. Someone had done it for her. On the floor and in the flight chairs laid ten people, dead or unconscious.

She quickly checked the first one. He was dead! The next one, Monzor himself, barely alive, was not moving. Someone used full stun force from a blaster on them!

Immediately going to the console, she opened the bay doors. Then into the speaker, "Mr. Henderson, I have ten bodies up here. Any down there?"

"A few seconds of static, then Mr. Henderson's voice came over her communicator, "This is not being quiet, ma'am, but yes, there's over a hundred down here. I have no idea where they came from. Some may be alive yet."

"I think we have only seconds, Mr. Henderson. This ship is going to blow. We'll have to deal with them later."

"I agree, ma'am!" I'm heading for the armory now."

"Judy, report! What's in your section?"

Over her communicator came Judy's voice. "Only bodies, ma'am. People we don't know. Going below the plates now."

"Good girl!"

Ana heard the lift door open behind her. Thinking somehow it was Mr. Henderson, she whirled around. "I thought you were checking…" Suddenly her heart stopped. She couldn't move! In front of her was Captain Craine with a blaster. She saw hers on the console five feet away. Why did she get careless and leave it there? While her mind calculated the distance, she heard the deranged voice of Captain Craine gloating.

"I thought it was you coming through the airlock. They left me here to die like the others. No witnesses they said."

Over the speaker interrupting him was Parker's voice. "We're inside. Have George with me. Funny how he recovered so fast. The shuttle is secured. Where do you want these positive pods? I don't plan on taking them into the gravity zone."

Captain Craine smiled. "Now that's nice of him. Thought I

would have to spacewalk over. Must be going! You guessed it, time is short!" Laughing, he squeezed the trigger.

Anticipating, Ana leaped for her weapon. The blast on narrow band for maximum effect missed. Her hand closed around the handle when the second blast reached her, but the space chairs took most of it. She had fallen down behind them. She still received enough of the blast to render her unconscious.

Captain Craine, unaware how successful he was, retreated. She had her blaster, no sense in pushing fate, he thought. He had his shuttle. He could escape the hell fire he knew was coming.

The sudden strain on her back opened her wound more, and the bleeding became pronounced. She felt herself falling deeper into the darkness inside. "She can't do this! The ship is in danger! It needs her!" Too late, she found herself floating out of her body. She saw the lift through her inner eyes indicating the lift was on the lower deck.

"Let him go," a voice said behind her.

Turning, she saw the floating blue essence of George.

"Mid-ship, the shuttle bay, I believe four proton bombs are rigged to explode. Tricky set up, but I think our Mr. Henderson can figure it out."

She only partially heard him while she struggled to get back into her body. She pushed hard against the waves of blackness trying to force her out. She felt her body moving. Then she heard her voice. It sounded low and distant coming over the speakers, "Mr. Henderson…Mr. Henderson…Shuttle bay…Four…Four proton…" Then she plunged into the soft darkness.

Below, the bay doors opened, and a small shuttle moved out into the starlit night with a full reservoir of fuel.

Dimly she heard the lift door open. Then Parker's voice, "Gees! What happened in here? Captain! Captain Mc Clure! Are you in here?"

George found her, "She…She looks dead, Doctor." He touched her and quickly pulled back.

Parker shoved him aside. He took a stimulate syringe from his med-bag and injected it into her black body, "She's not dead yet!"

George, pointed at the large red spot on her uniform, "Look! She's bleeding!"

"Yeah, I told her she would!" He sent another jolt of epinephrine into her body. "But that's not what knocked her down. This looks more like a blaster handiwork. They must have their toys."

Inside, Ana saw the bright light coming toward her. She ducked to avoid it. She felt secure. She didn't want to come back. Then Parker's second bolt of light was more direct shattering her blackness. It left behind a shower of sprinkling pain.

She heard Parker's voice become louder. "She's coming back! I told you she wasn't dead!"

Ana blinked and looked up to see George and Parker standing over her. She was embarrassed until she remembered the proton bombs. She rolled over and tried to stand.

Parker pulled her back. "No, you don't! Not, until I've checked you!"

Resisting, she struggled to get the words out, "Bombs…Proton bombs in the shuttle bay!"

George, recalling, said, "Yes, by the other pad. There was a pile of something there!"

Mr. Henderson's voice came over the communicator on Ana's belt. "Found them! They're ready to blow in one minute. No time to figure out the sequence, I'm sending them out behind the shuttle!" He manually started the drive on the center one after he pointed it toward the open bay door. "There they go! I wouldn't want to be on the receiving end of that. Recommend closing the bay doors and raising the shields. It wouldn't hurt to move out of the EM Unit."

Ana, sitting, softly said, "You heard him! Think you can do that, George?"

George, offended, went to the console and flipped a few switches.

Over the communicator Henderson's voice confirmed, "Bay doors closing!"

"Now the shields, and the engines," Ana continued, "We need to put some distance from it!"

George started to pull the power lever when a panic voice came over the communicator. "I found it! I found it!" It was Judy from below.

Ana, holding her side, staggered to the console. She pressed a few buttons and switched to the ship's speakers overhead. "Found what, Judy?"

"The explosive device! It's on the fuel storage tank!"

"Calm yourself! What does the timer say?"

"Forty-five seconds! It's going to explode in forty-five seconds."

Mr. Henderson came on line, "On my way!"

"No time!" Ana said, "Stay on the com.! Judy, describe the package to him! How many filaments?"

"None! It's sealed!"

"Can you remove it?"

"I don't know. I'm scared!"

"Try!"

"Have it! I have it! What now?"

"Mr. Henderson?"

"Trash evacuation. Should be just above her!"

"Hear that, Judy! Trash evacuation! Tell me when it's in!"

Ana's hand went to the trash capsule expulsion switch. It had its own power unit. It was meant to direct trash into the sun or some similar source. It was a way to rid the ship of contaminated matter produced by the ships engines, and the like.

Mr. Henderson yelled over the speaker, "Ten seconds and counting!"

"Thanks, we all wanted to know!" The doctor said with his usual sarcasm.

"Move it, Judy," Ana said, "Eight seconds. I need a couple to get rid of it."

"Now! Now!"

Ana flipped the switch. She waited two seconds, then she closed the shields, "Hang on!" She yelled. "This could be rough!"

The first explosion came from the package expelled from the trash container. It rocked them slightly. When the four proton bombs exploded, the proton wave sent the EM Unit and the ship into motion. Ana already had the ship moving. It cleared the EM Unit by millimeters before the unit started to roll.

Only one impulse engine was responding. She could not put any distance between them and the round EM Unit. They were running from the tumbling unit seeking them out!

Doctor Parker was staring at the aft screen. It was completely consumed by the EM Unit. "Holy gees, woman! Can't you veer away from that thing?"

"Could if I had more room, or more power!" She yelled and kept hitting the second impulse engine button. "Nothing! Nothing works!"

Mr. Henderson, coming off the lift, looked up at the screen, "How are we doing?"

Ana, not looking up, "Holding our own, but any slight lost in power, and we're part of the EM Unit."

Mr. Henderson moved toward the console, "I'm surprised you have anything. It's not like them to leave such an obvious escape open."

He pulled back the half-opened panel. Inside he found George sitting in the middle of a pile of torn filaments. His eyes were in a hypnotic trance staring at the sparkling filaments in his hands. "Here's your power source! Parker, get down here, but don't move him until I get these filaments connected!"

Carefully reaching around him, Mr. Henderson, with gloved hands picked up the two filaments. He bared them slightly and pressed them together.

Doctor Parker upon seeing George, yelled, "Gees! His hands are burning. He started to pull the filaments out when Mr. Henderson stopped him.

"Let me disconnect them first. He's carrying a lot of juice!"

Quickly Mr. Henderson had them cut, and George fell into Doctor Parker's arms. Mr. Henderson lifted him out of the console, and then climbed back in. Pulling more filaments around, he placed them together, "There, try the port side!"

Ana, above, pressed the second button, the ship responded. It immediately veered off to the left allowing the EM Unit to tumble out of sight with the proton wave. She accelerated until she was beyond the wave, then she turned and followed the EM unit. Picking it up on long range, she placed the coordinates into the computer. Satisfied, she sat back to relax.

Mr. Henderson came out from under the console saying, "It's a mess down there."

"How much time?"

"To repair it?" He asked. "Don't know the extent of the damage. I think you better be happy with the impulse power for a while."

"I want the EM Unit," Ana said.

"What for? We will not be traveling in any worm holes."

"It's a good offensive weapon."

"We don't know the extent of the damage it can do."

"It doesn't seem to be permanent. I think it might be ideal until we can figure this out."

Mr. Henderson moved toward the lift. "I'll set the positive pods. It will have to be done manually until we can get the board up." He looked at Parker placing the unconscious George in the flight chair.

"Had to put him out," Parker said. "His hands are completely burned. Don't know if I can save them."

"Try doctor! He deserves that," Ana said.

Doctor Parker nodded. Then turning to Mr. Henderson, "I didn't bring the board only the pods. There's only so much one can carry even in zero gravity. Now, if you two could give me a hand, I have people dying here who could use our help."

Judy stepped out of the lift and looked at the people on the floor. "There's hundreds below. I didn't check them. They…They looked dead."

Ana, taking charge, yelled, "Snap out of Judy! They were hit with a blaster! You stay with Parker and me! Mr. Henderson, go get those pods in position!" She pulled back more on the impulse power. "We'll follow the EM Unit until you're ready."

Mr. Henderson nodded, and disappeared into the lift.

Doctor Parker was already moving the people on the deck. He placed those alive closer together, and injected them with stimulates, then grumbling under his breath, "Could have used his strength. Your useless, ma'am! That leaves only us two."

Ana, ignoring him, asked, "How many are going to make it, Parker?"

"Of the ten here, maybe seven," he said, "Here!" He handed Ana his medical belt. He took Judy by the hand and started for the lift. "You stay with them! If they start to slip away, give them one push of the stimulate syringe. Don't over-do it!" Pushing Judy into the lift, he said, "Now, young lady, show me where the others are!"

Ana, moving to the floor beside her patients, tried to ease the pain coming from her side. Something was very wrong there, but it would have to wait. She allowed the blood from the opened wound to seep into her uniform.

Alone, she watched them slowly recover. She knew exactly what they were going through. Only one reversed. She watched his body go limp. Immediately she pushed the plunger. The injection entered the body without disrupting the skin. The young man erupted into a spasm. It worked, he was moving again.

Mr. Monzor, recovering first, sat up. His face became white upon seeing Ana.

His fear was apparent until she touched his arm. "It's okay, Monzor. I'm not here to hurt you."

"Where...Where did you come from?"

"Long story, I need to know what happen to you after the space station was attacked by the EM Unit."

His head was still spinning. "I'm not sure," he shook his head. "Fires started everywhere. Then the automatic extinguisher took over to remove the oxygen and smoke. Some of us passed out. I was one of them. When I woke, everything was dark except a few emergency glows.

I knew people were hurt. Some were killed when they were caught in areas requiring power. Others without life support died quickly. A little warning would have saved a lot of them."

"Where did you go?"

"Don't know," he said. "The only thing we could pick up was your ship and the Beta shuttle. Everything else was gone."

"Star Base Eleven?"

"Nothing! Like we fell in a hole or something."

Suddenly over the speaker came Doctor Parker's voice. "You wouldn't believe who we found down here. Your two missing security officers the High Achievers set adrift."

Mr. Monzor nodded, "Yes, we found them when we came back out of the black pocket."

"How long were you inside the pocket?"

"Don't know exactly, maybe four hours. All systems were down. I'm not even sure we were in a pocket. When nothing works, you can imagine anything."

"You were gone all right, the question is, where?"

"Coming back was even weirder, or maybe my eyes were adjusting. Like the bulkhead would disappear one second and then reappear. I saw people walk through them. In fact, we lost two people who walked right through the skin to the outside and found themselves without life support. The rest of us didn't dare move. None of us!" Monzor emphasized. "All we could do was watch them die. It was horrible."

"How long were you in the transition period?"

"Hard to say, eternity then, but probably ten minutes. We didn't know if we would fall through the deck and join the two outside or not!"

"Did anyone try to rescue them?"

"Not until later, I told you! We didn't dare move! We heard their screams! Their pleas for help, but we couldn't do anything. We watched them drift until the bulkhead became solid."

Ana, having a hard time believing, asked, "You mean you could see right through the bulkhead?"

"That's what I've been trying to say. We could see the outside and the inside at the same time. The fabric in the walls fluctuated in thickness from the light framework with nothing but space in it to full thickness. We could see the stars outside like we were floating in space."

"Your life support?"

"It didn't seem to affect that as long as we didn't move. Like I said, if you walked through the skin, you lost it."

"You said this fluctuation last ten minutes?"

"I don't know, maybe longer, but that's not all. We drifted back and forth twice since then. Not as severe, and we've always returned in a few minutes. It was like an earthquake after shock. We felt the station shake for hours after each one. Everyone wanted off!"

"What about the ship here?"

"No," he replied. "It was like we were in a warped part of space. When the ship moved out of it, it wasn't affected again."

"When you were in the pocket, did the ship try to move out of it?"

"It could have! We all felt this, but if it did, it probably would still be there. No, our only way back was to stay in the pocket until it returned to normal. When we did, your ship moved out of it, and wasn't affected anymore."

"So why did you all leave the space station?"

"Like I said, no one wanted to stay. Not until things settled down. Good thing too! When the electron wave hit, it took the station way out of orbit. I have no idea of its path now."

"Did you know the station blew up in the process?"

"It wouldn't have surprised me, but it wasn't the wave that did it."

"I didn't think so, probably the same ones who did this."

Mr. Monzor nodded, "My security detail, all ten of them!"

"Why?"

"I don't know. I think somebody didn't want witnesses to the wormhole experiment."

"Why did they wait until you were off the station before destroying it?"

"I think that was Captain Cranes fault by offering his ship."

Ana interrupting, "His ship?"

"Why yes, he was the only high-ranking officer in Star Fleet Command we had here. You know none of us can take charge of a Starship."

"He just took over?"

"Actually, he went a little crazy, but we thought it was the pocket affecting him. Anyway, the moles held off exposing themselves until we were in a nice tight bundle aboard your ship. You know, the space station, with so many places to hide, would have made it almost impossible to control everyone."

"Then you didn't know they blew up the station?"

"Not until you told me. All of it?"

"No, only the life support, and control center, at least as far as we could tell. The whole top section blew, but the lower half appeared to be intact."

"Probably where they went," Monzor said.

"Who?"

"The moles after they blasted us."

"Makes sense. We saw the Beta Shuttle leaving when we arrived. No shuttle could make it to Star Base Eleven without extensive life support."

"With ten aboard, no shuttle could carry enough supplies."

"What about Craine? How did he miss the blasters?"

"Like I said, he went crazy. He discovered the EM Unit coming back. Worked the ship around the electron wave, and found the unit sitting by itself waiting for us."

"Why did he bring the ship into the EM Unit? You didn't have positive pods?"

"I don't know. He wasn't rational. I think he thought he was on his ship. He was going to take the EM Unit, enter the worm hole, and complete the experiment."

"He couldn't face the failure?"

"More, when no one responded to his commands, he flipped out. He ran from the Bridge yelling, set the pods! Set the pods! A minute later the door opened. We thought it was

Captain Craine returning, but it was the ten moles. They fired point blank, taking us all out."

Ana touched her communicator, "Mr. Henderson, are the pods in place?"

"All but one keeping that. I have an idea how to retrieve the EM Unit."

"Did you pick up on Monzor?"

"Yes, interesting, I agree with him. The moles have to be at the station."

"Craine?"

"Probably heading that way if he survived the blast. He'll need supplies too."

"Parker, what's your status?"

Most are recovering, but this ship wasn't built to handle this many casualties. I have the whole second deck laid out with bodies."

"Life support?"

"Without more supplies it's hard to say. Like I said, the ship wasn't built to cycle this much."

"We'll have to get more. You hear that Mr. Henderson? Better make your list."

"Yes ma'am! We may have to fight for them."

"Didn't plan it any other way."

Suddenly the long-range scanner began to ping from the console. Ana moved slowly while holding her side. She brought herself up into her space chair and flipped the outside camera on. She pressed her communicator. "I have the EM Unit in sight Mr. Henderson. We can use that idea now."

"I'm placing a power pack to the positive pod. Then flipping the power pack to ship control, you can stabilize the spinning EM Unit when it attaches itself. The remote will be coming though auxiliary two. We'll use the torpedo tube to launch."

"Ready anytime you are. We're as close as we want to be." She began adjusting the ship's speed to correspond with the spinning EM unit. Coming below the screen, a red streak shot out toward the EM Unit. The torpedo tube thrust took the positive pod almost to the spinning unit. Then the power pack took over.

"Activate the pod," Ana said.

"Did when it left the ship."

"Right on target," Ana confirmed. "Contact! Lock! Using the power pack, easy…Bringing it back…Slowing…Got it! Ready for attachment, but we need the last pod before we attempt it."

She heard a muffled voice, then she saw a spacesuit with a thruster moving toward it. "Is that you, Mr. Henderson?"

"Yes ma'am! Have your pod in a moment."

"You were out a little early, Mr. Henderson."

"Trying to save some time. We're going to need it at the space station." Mr. Henderson retrieved and deactivated the positive pod from EM Unit. It was no longer spinning. He towed the pod back to the ship.

"You think they're going to blow it up?"

"I would if I had my supplies, and suspected we survived."

Mr. Monzor interjected, "I don't believe they could know that. We were not aware of your survival before the takeover. They would have to assume they completed their responsibilities."

Ana, watching Mr. Henderson entered the lock, "Craine knows, especially after we sent him the little gift."

Mr. Henderson moved through the lock, dragged the positive pod back inside, "I'll have this in place in five! She's right Monzor! He knows Judy and I am alive. Yes, I say he is the unknown factor here."

Ana, knowing Judy was on line, "Judy, have you been copying?"

"Yes ma'am."

"Do you have any walking security officers down there?"

"Yes," Judy replied, "A few of them seem to be able to move."

"Good, take two and show them how to activate the positive pods after they place them into position. Then put them on the com."

"Yes ma'am! On my way! I will report when we are in position!"

"We should be ready when you are, Mr. Henderson."

"Good! I'm about there. Sure, would hate to move this in gravity."

Ana waited a few moments before she brought the ship around. She edged the ship in closer to the EM Unit. This one was bigger than the shuttle. It didn't allow room for error."

Mr. Henderson, placing the positive pod, "Could have use the shuttle on this!"

"Are we ready, Judy?"

"Everyone is in position, ma'am, counting off, one!"

"Two!" A security officer said in another ship location.

"Three!" The second officer said.

Then Mr. Henderson replied, "Four, ready here!"

Ana slowly brought the nose inside the ring. "On my count then! Four, three, two, hit!"

The four positive pods came alive, and the ship jerked into place. Like a small earthquake, a jolt, and everything in the ship shifted to the upper right.

Ana, finding her feet, "Okay, so I was off a bit. Everyone survive, Parker?"

"As far as I can tell. You do make it hard to close wounds, ma'am."

"Thank you, Parker."

Mr. Henderson secured his positive pod, "About done here, on my way up. I still don't know what you plan on doing with the EM Unit."

"After all we've been through with it, we couldn't just leave it. Though, seriously the fact they want it destroyed makes' it valuable to us."

"I agree ma'am!" Mr. Henderson said entering the Bridge, "Now for some supplies."

"Yes!" Ana said reaching for her communicator, "But we have a bigger problem." Then into her communicator she said, "Parker! Judy! To the Bridge!" Then back to Monzor she asked, "Have you ever use a thruster pack?"

"Only during training school."

"Good, it will help," Ana said. Mr. Henderson, can we get the main drive working, and maybe some fire power."

"Don't know on the fire power, but maybe the main drive if I can figure out that mess below the console."

"Try for the fire power to if you please," she said.

Mr. Henderson started taking the panels off the bulkhead. He stopped after the second one, "Like I figured, they melted all the filaments. We'll have to make up another bank for the lasers."

"Time?"

"Two days' minimum."

"Can't give it to you, main drive?"

"See in a second," he said, and slipped below the console. "Maybe something here, if I don't get fried."

Doctor Parker with Judy behind him, entered the Bridge, and asked, "Is this really necessary? I have two hundred people who need me below."

"Sorry, wanted to keep this private. How many able bodies can you have say in two hours?"

"What do you mean by able? Barely walking, or able to go into combat?"

"The latter, Doctor!"

"Cold, are we not, ma'am?"

"The number please!"

"Maybe forty for your purposes."

"And the rest?"

"Will need a week or so. They don't seem to be made out of your fiber, ma'am."

"Give them to Judy. Now that you are in such a hurry please take another look at my side. I need to be functional in one hour. Up to then it can rest."

"You want me to anesthetize it again?"

"Yes, for about an hour," she said, "For now do what you need to."

"Bare it!" Parker said in a crisp tone.

Ana looked around quickly, "Maybe something more private."

"Gee, God almighty, Woman! There isn't time. Didn't you hear well? I've got people dying below!"

"Mr. Monzor coming to her rescue, "The station had a full medical complement. We brought them all aboard."

Doctor Parker glared at him, "Yes, now you have only two nurses! They're the reason I'm here!" He growled.

"Sorry, I didn't know," Mr. Monzor said and shrunk back.

Doctor Parker fixed his gaze back at Ana, "Well?"

"All right! All right! Everyone face the bulkhead! Any of you I catch turning around is going to wish he hadn't!"

Mr. Henderson, grinning, "And I thought you lost all your

modesty years ago."

"Shut up, Mr. Henderson! Just fix the damn main drive! The rest of you not doing something here go below. You can give those nurses a hand, but report back to Judy in the shuttle bay in one hour."

All except Mr. Henderson and one security officer ran for the lift.

Doctor Parker yelled after them, "Hold it! Don't blame you for running but take the three bodies with you. Put them in the torpedo launch area with the others."

Mr. Monzor, directing, started to go with them.

"Hold it, Monzor! You stay! I told you I want a private meeting here." Ana nodded toward the security officer, "You help the others. Monzor, give Mr. Henderson a hand."

The security officer, seeing his chance, quickly followed the others. The door closed, and the lift disappeared.

"Is your modesty protected now, ma'am?" Doctor Parker asked.

"Yes Doctor, you may proceed!" Ana dropped her uniform and fell to the floor. She lay barely conscious with the gaping hole in her side showing her intestine. Blood quickly began to ooze from the ten-centimeter hole. She tried to hold her focus. She was slipping out into the darkness until she felt the sting of the doctor's laser repairing the wound.

Doctor Parker had dropped to his knees. Irritated, "Yee gods' Woman! What were you thinking? You want this to get infected? It's not going to close properly this time. You go opening it again, it will have to stay open. You hear me?"

Ana could feel the darkness taking hold as the pain drove her out. She could no longer hear Doctor Parker's voice.

12 Alpha Twelve

Slowly she began to hear Mr. Henderson's voice talking to Parker in the background. He sounded like he was in the next room, but she knew he was standing right above her.

"You cannot use that. We need her conscious for a few minutes first. Then again in two hours."

"Why, so she can destroy what's left of her body?"

"Knowing her, you better do something more durable the next few hours anyway."

Doctor Parker looked up at Judy, "Then get me the barbaric stuff! You'll find it in my locker!"

Judy stood and looked at him. Her face was asking what.

"The damn tape, girl! The damn tape! Haven't used it in years. I usually have more cooperative patients."

Judy stumbled backward slightly. She didn't want to leave Ana.

"The tape!" Doctor Parker yelled in a rough voice. "Get along and bring her another uniform! This one is blood soaked!"

Judy turned and ran for the lift. The door closed, and the room remained silent. Doctor Parker took out a blade and began cutting away the rest of her uniform.

Mr. Henderson dropped down beside Parker to help, "How much blood has she lost?"

"Who knows?" He took a capsule from his belt, placed it in his injector. He shot the contents into her femoral artery. "There, that should give her enough electrolytes to keep her functional. You did want her functional?"

"Yes Doctor, the next few hours are critical."

"Hympt!" Parker continued his repair job and allowed the silence to continue.

Monzor came over after he discreetly looked around. He stared down at her. "She is beautiful, isn't she, even unconscious."

Parker looked up. He quickly became irritated. "She can hear you, gentlemen. I'd recommend getting on with your work!"

Monzor, embarrassed, turned back to the console, and began to separate the filaments.

"Treat her nice, Doctor," Mr. Henderson said in a concerned voice, "She's done more than her share on this one."

Doctor Parker continued his repair, "Then you better make her slow down, or you won't have a Captain. She takes too many chances. It's like she's on some sort of death wish."

"If she hadn't, we wouldn't be here discussing it."

"You have a point, Mr. Henderson." He gave her another dose of epinephrine.

Slowly Ana regained conscious. She looked up at Mr. Henderson, then softly she said, "Didn't know you had a tender side, Mr. Henderson."

Quickly becoming embarrassed, Mr. Henderson stood, "Maybe I better be getting back to the main drive and the EM Unit!"

Ana, covering herself with her arm, "The EM unit?"

"You said you wanted a weapon. It is effective. I think I can make it work manually. That's saying we can retrieve the control board. It works off the main drive. Of course, it will shut down everything."

Judy came off the lift. Her face was full of concern until she saw her Captain talking. "I…I brought the tape Doctor."

Doctor Parker, pleased with himself, smiled, "This should restrict your movement some." He took the tape and began wrapping her mid-section.

After the fourth time around, Ana stopped his hand. "Is all of this necessary?"

"It is for you!" He said removing her arm. He continued three more times before he allowed Judy to help her into the clean uniform.

Standing, she looked down at herself. She saw the bugle of tape pushing the fabric out. "Not very flattering, Doctor."

"We weren't going for looks, ma'am! You wanted to be functional. Now you're functional. If my job is done here, I have people who really need me!"

"Yes, but one moment, we need a long-range plan here. This ship cannot accommodate two hundred and fifty people. Most of them will have to go into the box."

"Well, we only have one psych tank," Doctor Parker said, "And twenty artificial animation boxes in storage. Even if we had the two hundred and thirty, you may have a rebellion on your hands. How would you store them? Where would you put them?"

Mr. Henderson stuck his head out from below the console, "Stack them!"

Doctor Parker shook his head. "They're not going to go for this. Besides, you can't stack the artificial animation boxes!"

"Why?"

"Gees!" Doctor Parker yelled, "You can't see them! How are you going to tell how they are doing? Besides, I think this conversation is useless. We haven't enough available."

Monzor interjected, "But we do! Not artificial animation, but Life Boxes. Survival gear, we have over six hundred in the port cargo bay. We were supposed to equip the fleet with them."

Mr. Henderson came out from below the console, "For survival inside, or outside the ship?"

"Both!" Monzor said. "No direct viewing plate, but it has a bow camera with a view screen. All the controls are inside. The skin is hard. It's supposed to be able to withstand a P-torpedo explosion. That's why no view plate."

Mr. Henderson smiled, "Then we could stack them."

Ana, interested, "But the controls are inside. What's going to prevent someone in the middle wanting out?"

"That's the beauty of it," Monzor said, "They open from the bow end. They can sleep in them, close them up, or be in artificial simulation, but they control the simulation."

Ana, not liking it, "So we can have people getting out anytime they want to, walking around the ship."

"They can unless Mr. Henderson takes the control away from them," Monzor replied.

Doctor Parker, not liking what he was hearing, "It's barbaric. You go taking the controls away, and you won't be having people climbing in them."

Mr. Henderson, testing, suggested, "We could put them out, then place them in."

"Don't you go counting on me to do this little deed for you. You want them out! You do it!"

Ana, interjecting, "Okay, we leave the control with them. First, we have to get the boxes." Turning to Mr. Monzor, "What else is in the port bay?"

"Most of the emergency life support equipment was stored there. Spacesuits and the like."

Mr. Henderson, thinking aloud, "That's where we well find our friends."

Doctor Parker moving toward the lift; "I have patients, ma'am!"

Ana nodded; "Yes, thank you, Doctor, by all means."

Judy's eyes were begging to go too. "I don't think I'm needed here."

"Yes, but remember this conversation is private. We don't need to panic people. Especially now." She looked at her wrist band. "At 0600 I want my forty volunteers at the shuttle bay."

Judy nodded and followed Parker to the lift.

Ana, coming back to Monzor, "We have twenty spacesuits, and six thrusters here. That cuts down our numbers."

"I thought Starships carried more spacesuits."

Mr. Henderson pulled himself from below the console, "Yes, ten on each shuttle, but we seem to be lacking those."

"Twenty will do," Ana said. "I plan on bringing back those shuttles. The other twenty will stay here to receive, unless we run into a problem."

"I agree ma'am," Mr. Henderson said, "The shuttles are priority!"

"I don't think the crates of Life Boxes will fit in a shuttle," Monzor said in an inquiring tone.

"We won't even try," Ana said. "We'll only use the shuttles for towing. Rig up lines and nets, try to get everything in one trip. This is your end of it, Mr. Monzor."

"Me?"

"Yes, you know where everything is. This is no time for mistakes. Cut the crates loose, tie a line, and tow them out. Use the net for the smaller stuff."

Mr. Henderson did not see his part, "What about the shuttles, ma'am?"

"I'll secure those!"

"Maybe I should take that part of it."

"No, we're on manual, or rather part of the ship is. We need you here to operate it. I don't think anyone else can. The main drive isn't working, and we are defenseless except for the shields."

Mr. Henderson accepted her reasoning, but he didn't like it, "Yes, but you should let someone else lead the charge for a change."

Ana smiled, "You do have some concern. I think you've been listening to Parker. No, I will retrieve the shuttles. More than likely they are both in the port bay."

"You might find one of our shuttles floating around," Monzor said. "We left them adrift after boarding the ship. No one wanted to go back. We didn't think about tying them down. Nor did we have the time with Craine threatening to leave us."

"I wouldn't plan on those," Mr. Henderson said. "The electron wave would have scattered them out beyond reach."

Ana nodded, "We'll have to get ours back. We'll use the thrusters."

Monzor, his face showing his fear, started to say, "I...I."

"Don't worry, we'll tow you," Ana said. "Only our personnel will have the thrusters. We'll tie up and use one thruster at a time. We'll burn half and move the next one up. That will give us maximum range from the station. Hopefully we'll be beyond any sensors they may have working. We need surprise!"

Mr. Henderson, agreeing, "Yes, you make good targets if they pick you up. Weapons?"

"Full complement, but our personnel only unless things get out of hand. When we have control, bring the ship in closer for the transfer using shuttles acquired for the towing."

"The plan is solid saying we achieve surprise."

"Mr. Monzor?" Ana asked as she turned to him.

"Ah…Okay, but I think we should have weapons."

"How many of you are trained in their use?"

"What does it take to point and fire?"

"In space, none! In a space station a laser miss directed could explode it!"

Monzor nodded, "I see your point. Okay, we follow you in."

"That will do it, Gentlemen," Ana said relieved, "Need any help up here, Mr. Henderson?"

"No, I can handle my end!"

"Mr. Monzor, you know what you are going after?"

"Affirmative! Everything is still packaged in the port shuttle bay."

"Then meet with Judy at 0600 with the nets and tow line. We will start the operation at 0700 saying I can find the station by then. That means everyone in spacesuits and attached."

Monzor smiled, "Yes ma'am!"

He started for the lift when Ana called after him, "Send Judy up please."

He nodded and entered the lift. When the door closed, the bridge became quiet.

Ana slipped up on her flight chair and leaned back. She tried to ignore the sudden sharp pain in her side. Letting it subside, she closed her eyes a moment. Only the snipping below the console broke up the silence.

She felt strange. It was like she was about to walk into something different. She allowed her mind to work through the plan. She didn't see anything in it that satisfied the feeling. Finally, breaking the silence, she said, "Mr. Henderson, what are your thoughts?"

From below the console, "About what, ma'am, the attack?"

"That and something else."

"Hmm…No, I am not picking up anything."

"Am I missing something?"

"No, the plan is good. There's nothing I would change. How do you feel physically?"

"Okay, I have felt better, but I can do this." Leaning forward, she flipped on the long-range scanner. "Time to get back to business."

"Reporting in ma'am," Judy said coming off the lift.

"Give me a hand up here. We need that station. See what you can find."

Judy swung up on her chair over Mr. Henderson and started working the dial. Her attitude was cold and hurting.

Ana, picking it up, "Do quadrants one and two. I'll do the other half."

"Yes ma'am!" Judy said. "Automatic may be easier."

"Everything is manual until Mr. Henderson can get it working."

"You wanted the main drive on line first, ma'am," Henderson said from below the console.

"Yes Mr. Henderson. This isn't critical up here. We'll find it, right Judy?"

Not responding, Judy kept her attention on the screen.

"Okay, what's bothering you? Let's get it out before we start."

Judy, letting a tear drop, "You ma'am! You…You keep me out of everything. You were hurt and didn't let me help. I could have…"

"Sorry, there wasn't time. That's not a good excuse, but that's all I can say. I didn't mean to exclude you. I know you are capable. I'm taking you with me on the attack. You will be second in command."

"You're…You're not taking Mr. Henderson?"

"Not on this one."

Wiping her tear, she smiled slightly. "Thank you, I'll do my best."

"Yes, I know you will," Ana said allowing her attention to drift back to the screen, when suddenly it started to ping. "There, I have it, sector two, seventy by twenty degrees starboard."

Judy immediately turned her scanner. It picked up the second ping. "I have it!" She said.

"Good, set the course, half impulse speed."

"Yes ma'am!"

"Why give them so much time?" Mr. Henderson asked from below the console.

"We need the time to. Maybe they'll have everything set out for us."

"I wouldn't count on that kind of luck."

Ana, suddenly tired, said, "Judy, keep us on course. Remember, take orbit fifteen. They can't see us visually there. If they're not using their sensors, we'll be home free."

From below the console, Henderson added, "And any further out will make the thrusters overwork. I still believe we shouldn't be giving them all this time. If it's all neatly packed, they could be gone before we arrive."

"No, Monzor said the crates wouldn't fit in the shuttles, which means they will have to break open the crates. That's going to take a while in weightlessness."

"Agreed, but time is in their favor."

Ana forced her body up, moved toward the lift, saying, "We'll stay on schedule. I'll be in the dome." She entered the lift and allowed it to take her down. Her mind knew it was something more. She wanted to reach Charlie inside. This feeling in the pit of her stomach wasn't going away. She needed information.

The lift stopped. She stepped off at the second deck and attempted to move down the hall. It was wall to wall people with most of them sitting and waiting. All of them were breathing their precious oxygen.

She entered the medical unit. Ten people were on makeshift beds on the deck, and four people occupied the fold up beds. These last four had their heads covered with a medical device used to control their breathing and heart rate. Parker was adjusting the dials on the panel while the other two nurses were attending those on the deck.

Ana worked her way through the people. Some of them gave way when they realized who she was. Finally, she reached Parker. "How many did we lose, Parker?"

Without turning, he said, "Twenty, counting the three

brought down from the bridge. If I can hang onto these four, there won't be any more!"

Ana, being shoved again, asked, "Okay, Parker, besides the normal ship's complement of twenty, how many people do we have?"

"Don't know," he responded, "We lost two of our own. I have one here barely making it. I don't know! You'll have to ask Monzor."

"Are these the only ones still down?"

Moving past her to the next patient, "Yes ma'am, if you will excuse me. Can we discuss this later?"

Looking around quickly, she nodded, "Yes…Of course." She worked her way out of the room. Taking a deep breath, she walked up the crowded hall. Yes, they needed the Life Boxes, she thought. Monzor didn't tell her the truth and neither did Parker. They both knew. Quickly she counted those in the hall. When she was over three hundred, she stopped.

For a ship built to handle twenty, they were on overloaded. At this consumption how long would it be before they swamped the equipment? Her mind came up with a rough estimate of two days before all of the oxygen in the compressed storage tanks was used. Then it would be what the machinery could produce. Yes, they were in trouble.

She took the lift down one more deck before she started for the dome. It was the same. People were crowding in everywhere. She felt herself suffocating. She knew it was in her mind. She could breathe, but they were taking her oxygen away. No! No! She must get herself under control. She just needed her chair and a moment to rest in the dome.

Seeing the hatch ahead, she moved faster towards relief. She needed her haven of peace and quiet. The noise threshold seemed to be rising. People were talking louder trying to be heard over the one beside them. They were probably talking about her. She didn't care. Pushing the hatch open, she entered her sanctuary.

It was dark. Only the stars from the dome gave off any light. She saw the outline of her chair. She started to move that direction, when someone screamed below her. She was stepping on someone.

"Wait your turn!" The person yelled. "We still have twenty minutes!"

"Close the door!" The voices were coming at her from all over the deck. The place was crawling with people. That was why everyone was in the hall. They were waiting to get in the dome.

Suddenly someone recognized her. "It's the Captain! It's the Captain!" The lights came up. People began moving out of her way.

She couldn't believe it. Her…Her place was taken over by them. Turning, she shook her head and left. She heard the hatch close behind her as she moved quickly down the hallway. Glancing at those waiting, she could feel the smiles in their faces. They knew she could do nothing about it. They were here. She would have to live with it.

Going up the lift, her mind began to focus on the attack ahead. Why she wanted to delay, she could no longer remember. It was something about a weird feeling. Enough, they needed action now! All she needed was for these people to realize they would out strip the facilities in forty-eight hours. Then they could watch murder and mayhem. No, only her security people would have the weapons. The lift opened. She entered the Bridge at the surprised look of Judy.

"I thought you were going to the dome."

"There's more room up here!" She barked, "Henderson, how long on the main drive?"

"You have it now," he said, "I'm starting on the EM Unit!"

"Good!" She swung up into her chair, pressed the communicator. "Mr. Monzor! Mr. Monzor to the Bridge immediately!" She waited a second, "All security personnel! Repeat! All security personnel to the Bridge!"

Mr. Henderson brought his head out, "Has there been a change in plans?"

Ana glared at him. "I say there has! Do you know how many people we have aboard?"

Henderson shrugged his shoulders, "Two hundred plus or minus."

"Try plus five hundred!"

Mr. Monzor, coming off the lift, tried to avoid Ana's eyes, "I understand you were below."

Turning toward him, she swung off her chair, "How many, Monzor?"

"What…People…Well a…You mean the ones breathing your precious oxygen?"

"Those are the ones!"

"Five hundred and fifty-three!" He said fast hoping she didn't hear it.

"Five hundred and fifty-three," she said in a surprised voice. "Judy! Mr. Henderson! Did you know about this?"

Judy, coming off her chair, "I…I didn't know how many. I thought there were a lot."

"Mr. Henderson?"

"Only what Monzor told us?"

"I guess that brings us back to you, Mr. Monzor! I'm sure you know the difference between two hundred, and five hundred and fifty-three on a ship of this size."

"Yes ma'am, but the life boxes will take care of it. Like you said earlier."

"Not if we only pick up two hundred!"

The security officers entered taking their positions around the Bridge.

"It's okay, Gentlemen, there's no threat from Mr. Monzor here. All of you will carry weapons. Only blasters will be used aboard the ship." She pointed to Ralph, the ranking security officers and four others standing near Monzor. "You people will accompany Mr. Monzor and select twelve of his people for the raiding party. Only you, and I mean only you will be armed. This will be full complement."

She looked at each one closely. "Any questions? Ralph?"

"Who are we attacking, ma'am?"

"The ones who killed our people,"

"Yes ma'am!"

"If there is nothing more, report to Judy in the shuttle bay in ten minutes!"

They all quickly snapped to attention, turned, and led Monzor off the Bridge.

Turning to Judy with the remaining security officers, "Outfit these men with blasters. Place on wide angle light stun. We only want to control them not kill them. You four will be working in pairs with two on each deck. Anyone who starts to panic take them out. George, are you feeling all right?"

"Yes ma'am." His voice was soft. It said not to pressure me. His hands were in bandages.

"Good, you stay on the Bridge with Mr. Henderson." Looking around, "Any questions?" Seeing none, she nodded to Judy. "Weapons!"

Judy opened the weapons' panel with her finger print, and code. She took out five blaster belts, giving one to each. Quickly the four security personnel left the Bridge.

Mr. Henderson reached in, took out a full complement belt himself, and handed one to Ana. Taking out five more, he said, "I'll distribute these personally!"

Ana, strapping hers on, "Good idea, Judy, yours!"

Judy, not saying a word, took hers, and put it on.

Ana swung up in her chair, "Okay, let's see if your main drive works." She pressed the siren indicating the ship was about to go into full thrust. She brought the throttle lever up and took a two-minute burn before she took it back down.

"Good," she said. "That should put us there in five. Mr. Henderson, reverse thrusters in two minutes. We don't want to pass it."

"Yes ma'am!" He said, climbing into his chair. He began working the impulse engines to bring them into the correct orbit.

Ana started for the lift, "Let's go, Judy. We have people waiting. Mr. Henderson, see you below in five. George, no one is to enter the Bridge except the three of us and Parker. Him, only in an emergency."

"Yes ma'am, emergency, have it!"

In the lift Ana started to say something to Judy. She changed her mind and looked back at the door.

The silence held a few seconds. Finally, Judy, unable to contain herself, said, "You're…You're not coming back, are you?"

Ana, startled, "Whenever did you pick that up?"

"From you," she said. "I know you feel it. Maybe you should not go on this one." Her voice became a whisper.

"That won't change things. Now that it has been said, it's out in the open. I can be more careful and avoid whatever it is that's supposed to happen."

"No," Judy said softly, "If you go, it will happen. I know it!"

The lift door opened. Too late to analyze it Ana stepped off and walked toward the shuttle bay.

Judy ran up beside her. "Let Mr. Henderson go!" She pleaded.

Ana stopped to face her. "Enough! The plan is set! If I trade places with Mr. Henderson, it weakens the plan. We both are in our correct positions."

"Yes, that's the problem."

"We will go with it. I will just have to be more careful. No more is to be said about it! I will not be having my people spooked before we start. Most of them have never been under fire, and only the seven of us have had any training."

People began to move closer hoping to pick up on their conversation. Judy noticed them first and nodded. They continued to walk toward the shuttle bay.

Monzor had his men in spacesuits floating out over the shuttle bay with lines attached. They carried several large nets and coiled lines. Monzor was talking to them over his wrist communicator when Ana and Judy walked into the locker room.

Ana raised her communicator. "No more over the regular channel. We go to com. four. Mr. Henderson, you pick that up?"

Over the speaker, "Yes, going to com. four," he said, "Coming down now. We have a twenty-kilometer orbit. All power is cut except emergency lift support. I didn't think we needed to advertise."

"Good! Mr. Monzor, you hear that?"

Monzor nodded.

"There will be no communication once we leave the shuttle bay until we make contact with whoever is on the space station," she said. "Everyone who heard that raise your right hand." She looked out the locker window and counted. "Switch to com. four. Now all those who can hear me raise their other hand."

Looking out again, she saw all of them with their hands' up. "Good!" Then turning, she took her suit out of the locker.

The five security personnel in their suits waited for their weapons before zipping up.

"Mr. Henderson's coming down with them," Ana said climbing into her suit. "You people will secure the port shuttle bay and protect the party outside working out the crates. Primarily we don't want any surprises. Judy here will direct this phase. This will leave me free to take care of the unexpected and coordinate with Mr. Monzor. Judy will show you the positions we must control to give us the most protection. I don't need to tell you to shoot first and ask questions later, any comments?"

Before they could answer, Mr. Henderson entered. He gave each his belt. Immediately they inserted the laser weapon into the suit. After lifting their thruster packs in place, Mr. Henderson began the process of checking them out.

Ana, inside her suit, took her laser. She fixed it in the forefinger of her right glove. "Locked!" She said.

Then over her communicator she continued, "Lasers gentlemen! Check the safety! Thrusters one at a time! Switch when half empty. Judy will be going first, and I will go last if necessary. When we reach the space station, break off to your spots. I will take Mr. Monzor's group into the bay. Okay, let's go!"

They zipped up and filed into the airlock. Mr. Henderson placed the last thruster and turned to Ana. He lifted hers' into place and secured it to her suit. "Careful out there. No hero stuff!"

She looked back at him, "You too?"

"Just be careful!" He wanted to say more, but he thought better of it.

Ana, letting it to slide, "If we find the Alpha Shuttle, I'll have Judy bring it back with the EM board before we start the towing."

"Yes, the most vulnerable part of the plan is the towing with everyone strung out. It would be wise to have a weapon. No telling what they may have working in there."

Ana smiled, zipped up her suit. She gave Henderson one last look and entered the airlock. Yes, she knew they were vulnerable, but something about the EM Unit as a weapon bothered her. It was all they had. Good strategy says to use it if necessary.

Pushing the emotion deeper inside, Ana opened the airlock and floated out into the shuttle bay. Everyone was in line with Judy moving toward the bay door. Giving her thruster a slight nudge, she moved into her position behind the last of Mr.

Monzor's crew. She needed to be in position to retrieve anyone breaking free of the line.

Deep down, she still did not trust all of Monzor's people. There could be another mole. One who is willing to die or survive with the others. "The most dangerous kind and the hardest to dig out," she thought.

She took one last look back. She saw Mr. Henderson's worried face behind the airlock. "Yes, he felt it. No, shake it off," she said to herself, "Must concentrate on the mission." Looking back again, he was gone. He probably left to set up for the EM board. Her mind wondered why this would upset her.

Moving out the bay door, she felt them closing. Suddenly her 'Being' was immersed in deep emotions of loneliness and desertion. Only their forward movement kept this emotion from surfacing. No one was looking back, only forward at the small burnt out space station ahead. It became outlined when it passed in front of a star.

Now it was the group. It became the ship. I must stay with them or be lost forever in the darkness. A magical line was drawn between the ship and the tiny object ahead. If you veered from it, you would find yourself heading into the darkness. The…The endless darkness. It was an illusion because she knew the ship without lights or transponder working, was lost to them. Going into orbit, it was no longer where they left it. Even the space station was moving. Without their thrusters they would have lost that by now. One of the first things a space cadet learned was the law of constant movement.

She watched Monzor's men. Their gloved hands gripped tightly to the line although each was hooked on mechanically. They all trusted and believed the line to be the reality. Lose it, you will find yourself alone.

Their whole movement reminded her of a school of fish moving through the vast oceans on Earth. I must stay with the group. The group became the order having its own existence. Their minds were unable to cope with the thought of being left alone, and slowly dying by themselves when their life support failed. She wondered how many would do it quickly to get it over.

Judy motioned for the next thruster. She could feel the movement in the line causing tension. One man started to bolt, but he quickly calmed himself when the line took on direction again. Yes, they must have direction. The school of fish must keep moving. It didn't matter who was leading or even what direction.

The space station became larger taking on a new meaning in this ocean of emptiness. It began to take the place of the group. Focusing, they no longer perceived it as dangerous. It moved, yes, but it was bigger increasing their focus. The school of spacesuits, needing the anchorage, eagerly looked that direction.

Two thrusters move toward her. Taking the line, they

reversed the burn direction. Suddenly the group lined up the opposite direction. She found herself in front of the group as they approach the station. It was bigger now, much bigger!

It was working. They were going to make it. The group was focusing on it, when suddenly everything went wrong. A laser fire from the upper right corner of the shuttle bay struck one of her men with the thruster pack on.

He doubled over causing his thruster to hit two people beside him before the automatic switch kicked in to shut it off. The group responded with six lasers cutting into the framework where the fire came from, but it was too late for the group.

They were no longer balanced. The line began to tangle. Spacesuits collided, and others began swinging wide. Ana immediately cut herself loose continuing to fire at their assailant. She stopped when Judy with four others moved down into the shuttle bay to take up their positions.

She started to go back toward those above when she saw them passing her. Quickly hitting her thruster, she moved herself into position. Reaching out with her left hand, she took a bite on the line. She felt the strain on her bandage and the shooting pain in her back. Ignoring it, she locked onto the line. Slowly she began to brake their momentum. Finally, the whole group lay on the deck completely entangled in a configuration of lines and nets.

She watched them start the process of untangling themselves. Satisfied they would be okay, she moved on into the bay. Immediately she saw the Alpha shuttle on the fourth platform. It lay slightly on its side because of the broken strut. The airlock was wide open with cargo halfway inside. Yes, they caught someone packing to leave. Must be Craine, she thought, otherwise we would have picked up more laser fire.

She started to move closer when Judy angled in front of her entering the shuttle first. Satisfied it was empty. She came back out with a sheepish grin on her face.

Ana smiled, yes, this was going to be a problem. Breaking communication silence, she touched number four on her communicator. "Mr. Henderson, we have the port shuttle bay, took three casualties, sending them back with the Alpha shuttle and your board. Keep the shields in place, took one laser fire. Repeat, took one laser fire."

Monzor, having untangled himself, was breaking out the casualties. Others began helping. They brought the three toward the shuttle.

Ana motioned to Judy, "You'll be taking them back."

Judy nodded, and began pulling the remaining cargo into the shuttle to clear the airlock.

Right behind her Monzor eased the security officer who took the laser into the airlock. He looked back at Ana and shook his head. "Went right through him. Lost his air. What else, I don't know."

He moved back to allow Judy to take him in. The others in

better shape were placed in the airlock. Judy didn't bother taking them out but closed the hatch and lifted off. Moving easily out of the bay, she disappeared into the darkness.

Ana touched her communicator, "Judy is on her way with the causalities."

Monzor's men, finally free of the nets, began spreading them out. Not easy in no gravity, but they were accustomed to it. They began slowly disconnecting the huge crates from the bulkheads and lining them up.

One container of Life Boxes has been smashed opened, allowing the boxes to float off toward the ceiling. Monzor started to retrieve them when Ana stopped him.

"Let them go, Monzor. Concentrate on the full crates. I have a feeling we are short on time."

"Yes ma'am. It was probably our Captain Craine securing a box for himself."

"Let's not discuss it! We have no idea who is listening. There will be no talking unless absolutely necessary."

Monzor nodded and headed back down with the others.

Ana, turning, checked the security positions. All of her men were in place.

Yes, it was Craine. Long gone by now, she thought. She would be. He wouldn't take us all on. He had no idea how many lasers we brought with us. No, he would retreat. The one laser fire was to slow us down. He was probably heading for the starboard shuttle bay with a Life Box.

Touching her communicator, "Mr. Henderson, I'm moving inside. No contact other than the first laser fire." She didn't want to tell him where she was heading. By now Craine would be listening in on their communication. But more importantly where were the ten security officers from the space station? Craine knew, or he wouldn't be firing on us. One doesn't make his presents known if he has ten lasers looking for him. Her mind tried to reason this out while she worked her way through the first lock and headed down the hallway.

The emergency lights were on inside making the passage workable. Otherwise, the station was dead. These were the self-contain glow lights. They operated independent of the main circuit. They would last a year before they would start to fade.

Pulling the rails, saving her thrusters, she moved rapidly down the open hall. She felt the pull on her bandage and slowed some. No, she could not do this for long. She was progressing well until she met the emergency panel closing off her section. All the passages possessed emergency panels that came into play when the life support system was breached. It separated the station into sections.

This one didn't stop her. Someone had already cut a hole through it with a laser. Bigger then he needed. Yes, he was towing a Life Box. How many panels could he cut this size before his laser stopped functioning? She moved through two more panels. Each was the same. She knew the holes were slowing him up. He was heading for the starboard shuttle bay all right.

Suddenly Monzor voice came over her communicator. "Found the missing security officers. Thought they would be here."

Ana, thinking he needed help, "Where?"

"The emergency ward at the center of the space station. We have two hundred suspension units here. They're inside ten of them."

"Don't touch them! We'll deal with them later!"

"No need, someone has already been here. Each one has a laser hole through his chest."

"Nice, the other boxes?"

"Seem to be okay, but we don't need them. The Life Boxes are better, and we have enough of them."

Ana pulled herself through another hole. She could feel the warmth in the metal. She was getting closer. She had to be more careful. He has to know she's coming after him.

Mr. Henderson's voice came on line. "Monzor, are you at the very center of the station?"

"Yes, the very center."

"Then I would suggest looking for anything unusual."

"You think?"

"Just look! How are your men doing?"

"Had everything we need on line before I left. We're waiting for the shuttle's return."

"Shuttle's approaching now. I would suggest moving back toward the bay."

"Yes! Yes!" Mr. Monzor said, his voice becoming excited. "In a moment, I see something here. A…A black box. No…Looks more like a proton pod. Yes, it's a crate of proton bombs. Why would anyone bring that up here?"

"Don't touch it!" Mr. Henderson shouted over the communicator, "Is there a timer on it?"

"Maybe…" Pulling myself around it, "Yes! Yes! There's something that looks like a timer."

"How much time, Monzor?"

"Let me see…Hard to read this through the spacesuit. Should have made my last eye appointment. Looks like three minutes. No, less than three minutes. Two minutes, and forty-five seconds."

Ana set her timer inside the spacesuit, then pressed her communicator button. "Monzor, get out! Get out now! Judy! Judy, come on the com."

"Yes ma'am!"

"Take only what's hooked on and lift off! Leave a thruster behind for Monzor. Move away from the station at a right angle. Don't try for the ship!"

She pulled herself through another hole. It felt extremely hot. "Slowing, he can't be far," she thought. Then in the middle of the hall she saw the Life Box. She approached cautiously until she saw the hole on the other side. Smaller, yes, the man's laser was wearing down. She pulled herself through.

Then over the communicator she heard Mr. Henderson's voice, "Shuttle moving away from the starboard bay. Is that you, ma'am?"

Ana, feeling her whole world collapsing, turned back toward the Life Box. "No, Mr. Henderson, that's Craine!" Coming into the hall, she looked at the number on the bulkhead. "Monzor, I have number twenty-three here. How many bulkheads to the outside?"

"Four ma'am!"

She heard a thruster in the background.

"Better hurry," he said. "Forty-five seconds I believe, ma'am."

"Mr. Henderson, is the EM Unit working?"

"Board's in place."

"Hit the space station in twenty seconds."

"Have it! Good idea except you're in it, ma'am."

"It will save the others! I'm entering the Life Box now! Monzor, what are these holes at the one end?"

"Thrusters, ma'am. Not much range though."

"Thanks! Mr. Henderson maybe I can blast my way out of here during the transition."

"Understand, Monzor's clearing. I'm turning the EM Unit on in five."

Ana released the hatch at the opposite end from the thrusters and slipped inside. Tight, she didn't take the time to remove the thrusters on her back. She managed to close the hatch before the EM Unit started the vibrations.

Zipping open her spacesuit, she worked her fingers over the inside panel of the Life Box. Immediately it lit up. It read thrusters right and left. Placing her fingers on the buttons, she said, "Ready Mr. Henderson!" Nothing! "Ready Mr. Henderson!" Then she remembered she was not connected into the box. She started to search for the communication button.

After a quick glance at the time, she changed her mind. It read twenty seconds. She pushed the thruster buttons. She felt a slight resistance, but she was through something. In quick succession she passed through three more. She was free!

She saw something on the board reading, "Shields!"

Pressing the button, she felt the thrusters stop, and heard the movement of the metal umbrella closing the end of the box.

Suddenly she felt herself hurling out into deep space. The proton wave had hit her Life Box after the explosion. She didn't know it, but the metal shield took the brunt of the force. It melted, leaving a curled-up frame in its place. Doing its job, the life box only received a slight fusing on the corners facing the explosion.

She knew what was next. The explosion would contract. Pressing the thrusters, she felt the shield drop off and the box accelerate. "I need to put some distance from the center where everything will be in melt down," she thought.

Wanting to see, she looked for the outside camera. She felt the view screen. Yes, there must be an outside camera. Too bad she didn't have time to read the instructions on this thing. Finally, on the right side of the screen she found the buttons. After pushing the right one, the screen lit up. It only showed the forward direction. She didn't dare turn the box around to look at the space station. Each second away from the center was important. One may save her life.

She felt the box heating up even through her suit. Adjusting, she zipped up. She didn't want to chance a seam coming loose in the box. How much heat her suit can handle she knew. The box she didn't. It would have to be the box that saved her.

Feeling the heat building, she turned up the cooling system

in her suit. The heat still penetrated. She needed more distance! Suddenly the thrusters stopped. Looking through her faceplate, she could see the fuel indicator on the panel flashing red. Either she was out of fuel, or the heat melted the exhaust tubes. Drifting, she continued to move away from the center of the blast.

"It won't be enough," she thought, "Hard to keep my focus. It must be the box activating itself or the heat."

The outside camera continued to work. She tried to concentrate on it. Something big and ominous was approaching, or was she moving toward it. She was unable see the size. It blended with the darkness. Her mind locked in on a large starship, but it looked like a black asteroid. "It didn't have the shape of a ship," she said to herself. "Why did I think that?"

Coming closer, she could see the black slate rock covering the surface. The asteroid had to be twenty or more kilometers in diameter. These thoughts kept coming. She was going to crash on the asteroid or be consumed by the proton core. She visualized the box melting around her body. She knew there was no way to turn. The asteroid was too big. She was out of fuel.

What a wimpy box. Monzor called this a box of life. The new improved model, he said. She could give them a few clues. It was obvious none of them ever depended on it. Probably the one who tested it was part of a proton glow. They never did get his comments. "I have some! You hear me Monzor! I have some!" The rock was coming fast. She was not able to take her eyes off the screen or turn the panel off.

Suddenly the end of the asteroid closer to her opened. A huge mouth, big enough to swallow an entire space station, opened and engulfed her. The heat was gone. She found herself in total darkness when the door closed.

No, this was only a rock. She saw it! She was going to crash any second! She felt herself being thrown against the view screen. She stopped! See she stopped! Something was holding her! She didn't crash! Something…Something was holding her. The box animation wanted to take over. It was hard to concentrate. She felt herself drifting off. Reaching up she pressed the off button, but she was too late to stop the total effect. She was going to be out for a while. She knew it, but she felt safe. She was inside something big. It would protect her.

Continued to Bodhi Three - Asteroid

www.ingramcontent.com/pod-product-compliance
Lightning Source LLC
Chambersburg PA
CBHW032110180726
48284CB00002B/521